COOPER & PACKRAT

Mystery of the Missing Fox

By Tamra Wight

Illustrations by Carl DiRocco

ISLANDPORT PRESS

ISLANDPORT PRESS

ISLANDPORT PRESS
P. O. Box 10
Yarmouth, Maine 04096
www.islandportpress.com
books@islandportpress.com

ISBN: 978-1-939017-89-5
Library of Congress Control Number: 2015945267
Printed in the USA

Dean L. Lunt, Publisher
Front cover, back cover, and interior art: Carl DiRocco
Book jacket design: Karen Hoots / Hoots Design
Book design: Teresa Lagrange / Islandport Press

For my godsons,
Nick, Ty, and Matt—
who love a good adventure as much as I do.

Chapter 1

*A pair of foxes will have a litter of two to twelve kits,
usually in March or early April.*

"Careful, Cooper!" Summer's loud whisper came from behind me.
"Fresh dirt's been kicked out of that den. Something's gotta be living in
there!"

I turned to warn her with my eyes. I'd only known Summer since last
July, when she'd moved in to the old Wentworth house across the lake,
but I knew her well enough now to know two things: One, when she got
super-excited, her voice went up and up and up; and two, she got super-
excited a lot. Over big things and small things. And medium things.

But, she was right. There was a little more dirt outside the hole
than there had been a couple of days ago when we'd strapped my trail
camera to a skinny birch tree deep in the woods behind my family's
campground, and pointed it right at that opening. The kicked-out dirt
made a nice, flat shelf, even though the hole was in the side of a small
hill. Now, with the help of the trail cam's memory card, we'd get to see
what sat on it. So far, the motion-sensor camera had only snapped pictures of animals walking by: a fisher; a coyote; a skunk; and a fox. But it
hadn't captured what came and went from that hole.

I ran a hand through my short brown hair, and took a deep breath.
"I'm going in," I said.

I felt in my pocket for the little blue memory card I planned to
switch out with the one already in the trail cam. Hitching my backpack
higher on my shoulder, I parted the branches of the bushes we used as
cover. When I heard Summer take a step with me, I rolled my eyes.

"No," I said, "stay here, in case it's the fisher or the skunk."

Her brows came together, and she wrinkled her nose.

"So? I can do whatever you do—whatever *boys* do."

When I hesitated, she tugged her light blonde ponytail tighter through the opening in the back of her Red Sox hat and pushed up the brim to give me one of her please-please-please looks.

"Oh, c'mon. Just a little bit closer?"

Just like with my little sister, Molly, I had a hard time saying no to that look. "Fine, just be—"

Summer made the zipping-her-lips-shut motion.

I moved through the tall, thick bushes, parting their branches with both my arms, feeling them tug at my sweatshirt and jeans as if they didn't want me to go. On the other side, the forest floor was spongy-soft from April showers and littered with fallen trees covered in bright green moss. I carefully made my way to the cam, stepping only on the high spots, which were usually the logs. I'd learned the hard way that the low spots were deeper than they looked. I didn't want to sit through another Mom-lecture on the importance of taking care of my shoes, like I had last week when the mud had gobbled up my left sneaker.

Reaching the birch tree, I pulled back the two clips on the right side of the cam and quickly swung open the face of it to find the OFF button. I didn't want to record the hairs in my nose as I leaned over it to change the memory card.

A rustling sound filled the quiet forest air, like someone was crinkling paper. *Probably a mouse under the leaves,* I thought.

"Cooooper?" Summer whispered from behind me.

I turned my body very slowly toward the bank. A small, reddish-brownish face with two pointy ears looked out from the den opening. A set of curious black eyes met mine.

A kit! A red fox kit!

It was so cute! About the size of a small puppy, it had fur a little browner than that of an adult red fox, but the pointy ears, the black nose, the white line along its chin—there was no mistaking the markings.

Now I really couldn't wait to see what was on the memory card! I turned back to the cam, pushed the card in, and the camera released it. I pulled the card from its slot and shoved it deep in the pocket of my sweatshirt.

"Cooooper!" Summer whispered again.

I looked over my shoulder at the little hill and almost tripped over my own two feet as I turned around. Two kit faces, side by side! I shot a smile over my shoulder to Summer. One of the kits cautiously stepped out, and another face appeared in its place in the hole. I wanted to jump up and down and yell, "Cool! Three!" Instead, I stayed as still as possible, watching the kits, as the kits watched us.

One of the two in the den slowly moved out to stand next to the bravest of them all. It sniffed the ground with its little black nose. Then it sat on the dirt shelf like a dog, and, using its hind leg, scratched behind its ear while raising its nose in the air. The bravest kit pounced, and the two of them rolled around on the shelf, nibbling ears and noses, pushing at each other with their paws.

Another face appeared in the opening! Four? *Four!* Weren't they afraid? We were fifty feet away, maybe seventy-five. Not close, but hadn't their mother taught them not to—

The mother! I looked up and down the bank, and all around the woods. If she was around, she was well hidden.

What would she do if she knew we were here? She wouldn't abandon them, would she? I looked quickly at the kits, and sucked in a breath of air to see another reddish face added to the hole.

"Five!" Summer exclaimed.

Every kit froze, their eyes on us. We all looked at each other, like in a game of who's-gonna-blink-first. When the bravest kit's ear twitched, Summer giggled out loud. The sharp noise must have been one sound too many, because the kits scampered back into their den—three into

the main opening at the top of the hill, the other two into a smaller one halfway down.

I rolled my eyes. Summer might not always be the quietest, but she did love to nature-watch. And since I only saw my two best friends, Packrat and Roy, when the campground was open, May through October, it was cool to have a friend who lived only a short kayak ride or snowshoe trek across the lake.

I turned back to the cam, sliding the fresh memory card into the skinny slot and giving it an extra push to lock it in place. I turned the power to the ON position and closed the front.

"Sorry," Summer said, green eyes pleading with me to forgive her.

I smiled and pointed back to the den. One of the kits was already back, peeking out, curiosity winning over fear.

"C'mon," Summer whisper-coaxed. "Be brave."

A soft spring breeze blew again. The kit sniffed at it before taking a little bitty step. His left ear twitched. He took another step, sniffing the ground in front of him before taking one more, and then another. Now every inch of him, including the white tip of his tail, could be seen.

My radio crackled.

"Cooper? Where are you?" Dad's voice sent the kit scampering back into the shadows of the den again. "I've already notched the first tree."

Notched it? I frowned at the radio for two reasons: One, I'd forgotten the errand he sent me on; and two—I said, "Rule of Two, Dad. You have to wait for me."

"You're late." A pause, then, "I gave you strict orders. Grab my toolbox from the water-tower shed, and come right back. You promised; no detours. No collecting Oscar from his winter hibernating home."

Uh-oh. Dad was annoyed. No, actually, he was more like I-can-barely-talk-to-you-right-now mad.

"When I give instructions, and you're on the clock, I expect you to follow them like any other campground employee," he said.

I rolled my eyes. How many times had Dad set me up with a job *we* were gonna do together, only to ditch me halfway through to do what he called "more important stuff"?

"I'm sorry!" I snapped. "I'll go get it and be right there." And hopefully spy my three-legged frog awake and sunning himself on a rock, so I could bring him home and put him in Mom's garden.

"You didn't even get *there* yet?" Dad breathed a heavy sigh. "You know what? Just forget the toolbox. Come straight back! I never should have let you and your mother talk me into opening early for those reality-show camping people. Now we've taken reservations to fill the place, and if we don't get it open and looking good, we'll look bad on TV, and look bad to the campers and—"

There was a pause. Another heavy sigh. "Coop, I'm not discussing this over the radio. Just get back here. I need you."

Needed me? Ha! I turned off the radio and dropped it into my backpack without answering. *Only when there was work to be done. He never bugged me to fish with him. Or canoe.*

"Ready?" Summer asked.

"Ready."

I hung my backpack off my right shoulder as I stood, giving one last look over my shoulder at the fox den. One little kit face peeked from the opening.

"Stay safe," I whispered. "I'll be back."

If I'm not grounded for life.

Chapter 2

The average life span of a red fox in the wild is two to five years.

Hearing the faint roar of Dad's chain saw, my walk on the trail back to the campground turned into a slow jog. The scrunching of Summer's sneakers on the soft forest floor, and the occasional crack of a twig being broken, told me she was keeping up. My backpack bounced on my back in time with my steps.

This end of the trail came out next to our WELCOME TO WILDER FAMILY CAMPGROUND sign, and across from the campground gate. When we stepped on the dirt road, Summer picked up her pace to jog alongside me.

My breathing was heavy, my heart pumping fast. I didn't stop at the store, but kept going into the campground, down the road toward the lake and the sound of that saw. It was louder now, with occasional slows and squeals to it. Dad was cutting that tree without me!

I took a right at the second intersection. Summer turned to walk backward, toward the lake.

"I'm gonna . . . head home . . . okay?" she said between breaths, hitching her thumb toward the beach where she'd left her kayak. "I didn't check . . . in with my . . . dad yet."

I turned to walk backward too. "Sure. I gotta work the rest of today anyway."

She waved before turning and walking away.

I saw Dad's truck parked on the side of the road, about ten sites down. The roar of his saw cut through the quietness of the campground. Normally, we didn't open until May 15, but a couple of weeks ago, the director of the *Camping with the Kings* television show had called Mom with a cool question. The hosts of the show, Tom and Sue King and their five kids, were heading from a campground in Washington, DC, up to Quebec, Canada. Due to a late winter up there, they had some time to kill; would we like to be featured on their show?

At first Mom thought it was a prank call. She'd actually hung up on them! But they had called back and convinced her they were for real.

The catch? There were two things we had to agree to: One, whether the King family liked us or hated us, the show went on; and two, they had to check in to the campground May 1. That was two weeks earlier than usual. Mom was all for it. Dad was not.

"It's a struggle to open on the fifteenth every year!" he'd argued. "There's too much to do. Trees need to be cut, branches picked up out of the road, bathrooms and rental cabins opened and super-cleaned, picnic tables painted, boats brought to the water, flowers planted. And the water!" Dad had thrown his hands in the air. "We can't open the park without the water turned on."

"The weather has been unseasonably warm," Mom reasoned. "Campers are begging me to let them camp early, and I've agreed. A few groups are arriving today, and five or six more next weekend. I'd planned to put them on Maine Street, since the water is on there year-round. But why not just open it all up?" When Dad had started to protest, she'd held up a hand. "I think our campground is the most beautiful in Maine, don't you?"

"You know I do," he'd said gruffly.

Mom nodded. "The King family is into nature, boating, scenery, and people. They're going to love it here. And when they talk about us on national television, imagine how many camping families will see it! They'll want to camp with us! We'll be famous!"

That had done it. Dad agreed, but he'd been like an annoyed grizzly bear ever since, working long hours and grumbling every chance he got about only having two weeks to get ready to open.

Still, I was on Mom's side on this one. Opening the whole camp-ground on May 1 meant my best friend Packrat could be here as early as next weekend! And Roy right after that! The two of them were sea-sonal campers—campers who stayed weekends in the spring and fall, and every day during summer vacation.

I wonder what they'll want to do first? I thought, as I kicked a small rock down the road in front of me. *Fish? Canoe? Check on the loons? Look for the eagles' nest? Hey! Now I could show them the foxes!*

"Cooper!" Dad's panicked yell cut through my thoughts, making me stop short in the road a couple of sites away from his dump truck. "Move!"

I heard the word, but my brain didn't register it. *Move where? Back? Forward? Why?*

Suddenly, I felt strong hands on my back, shoving me to the side of the road. I landed face-first in a shallow ditch, my knee coming down hard on a rock, pine needles up my nose, dirt in my eyes.

I jumped up, rubbing my knee. "What the heck!?" I cried.

Through the red haze of my anger, I heard creaks and cracks. I looked up to see a five-inch-round pine slowly fall, twirling as it went. Based on the angle, it was gonna land right where I'd been standing.

Right where Dad was now. He must have stumbled and fallen in his rush to push me out of the way. He was on his hands and knees, head still down.

"DAD!"

His head came up. His eyes met mine.

"Get up!" I yelled. "Please! Get up!"

He looked back at the tree and froze. His hands began pawing the earth, feet scrambling to find a foothold. I moved toward him, but the first branch crashed to the ground, exploding between us. I threw my arms up around my head, but didn't take my eyes off my dad, who was frantically looking around. He turned to run away, but a second branch hit the ground right in front of him.

The tree trunk twisted toward Dad as it fell the last few feet. I lost sight of him in the green pine boughs and brown branches.

I heard a cry of pain. A smaller moan.

Then all was silent.

Chapter 3

*Both fox parents care for their kits during the first
months of their lives.*

"Dad!" I screamed, rushing forward, snapping the pine's branches as I struggled to get to where he lay on the ground. I crawled under the last few branches, too thick to break.

"Daaaad?"

I leaned over him. But he didn't answer. He was still. Very still.

I reached out a hand. Pulled it back. Was he? He couldn't be.

I touched his arm, but he didn't open his eyes. A terrible-sounding moan came from his lips. My throat felt like it was closing up.

"Help!" My voice didn't sound like my own. I raised my head and with as much force as I could, I cried, "HELP! Somebody!"

My phone! I reached in my backpack, pulled it out, and speed-dialed the camp's phone number. It rang once.

Footsteps were coming my way.

The phone rang twice. *C'mon, Mom, pick up—pick up!*

Summer's voice came from somewhere beside the tree. "Cooper!"

"Over here! It's Dad! He's hurt!"

"Don't move him!" she cried. "I'm coming!"

"Wilder Family Campground." Mom's voice, coming through the phone, all calm, friendly, and businesslike, made my eyes well up.

My mouth opened, but the word was breathy. "Mom?"

She gasped. "Cooper! What?" She was on Mom-alert.

Summer crawled the last few feet, as I had. My friend gently put two fingers on Dad's neck, between his ear and collarbone. One second passed. Two.

Mom's voice again. "Are you hurt? What's the matter?"

"It's not me, it's Dad." My eyes were on Summer, and when she breathed a sigh of relief, I did too. "Call 911," I told Mom.

Mom took in a sharp breath. "Quickly—what happened? The short version. They'll ask."

"A tree. It fell on him." My hand holding the phone shook.

"Is he . . . is he . . . awake?" Mom's voice sounded small and far away.

"No. But he moaned," I rushed to reassure her. "And Summer says he has a pulse."

"Okay. Stay with him. I'll lead the ambulance to you from the gate." A pause. "Tell him help is on the way." I heard her breath hitch.

"Tell him . . . I'm coming."

Later, they said the ambulance arrived in five minutes. It felt like fifty-five.

I'd put my hand in Dad's, the left one, because the right arm was bent at an odd angle. I held his hand tight, even though it was limp. Summer said his pulse was strong, and not to worry. But the tears in her eyes told me what her words didn't.

Somewhere in the back of my mind, I heard the sirens screaming, only to me they sounded like, *Yooooou. Yooooou. Yooooou!*

I'd done this. I hadn't cut the tree down or put him under it. But I hadn't paid attention on the work site. I hadn't come right back to help like Dad had asked.

I hadn't been his second in the Rule of Two.

I hadn't had his back.

Please, I prayed. *Please let him live. Let him be okay.*

An emergency medical technician cut through the branches and gently asked Summer and me to back up. When I shook my head and kept my hand in Dad's, he crouched down to look me in the eye.

"It's okay, son. You kids did a great job. We've got it from here."

He helped me up and led me through the broken and cut branches on the ground to stand by Mom and Molly.

"Is Daddy okay?" my six-year-old sister Molly asked, putting her hand in mine, much the way I'd done with Dad's.

Mom's arms crossed in front of her body. I stood as close to her as I could get. Molly leaned into both of us.

"He'll be fine," Mom said, a little too firmly. Her gaze fixed on the scene before us, she said, "Your dad's strong . . ." A pause, and then, "I don't understand. How could this—" Her voice cracked.

A small crowd had gathered. I could hear voices, whispering, or trying to. Where'd they all come from? We only had a couple of campers on Maine Street.

Why didn't Dad open his eyes?

The EMT who'd spoken to me had a hand on either side of Dad's head. Dad's neck was now in a white collar. Another, a woman, took his pulse, giving numbers to a third EMT who'd shown up in his own car. Dad's right arm had been wrapped tightly to a long, skinny, board-like thing, to keep it from flopping around. The lady EMT went to the ambulance and came back with a long blue board that kinda looked like one of our paddleboards. She laid it next to Dad.

"Get ready to roll him," she said to the head-holder.

She knelt next to Dad and, reaching across him, grabbed the cloth of his shirt and pants on his side, at his shoulders, and at his waist. She nodded to show she was ready. Head-holder said, "Watch the arm. On three. One, two, three."

She rolled Dad toward her, up on his side. The third EMT slid the board under him and they gently lowered him onto it.

His pulse was checked again. The EMTs secured him to the board with blue, seat-belt-like straps. I could already see a purple mark on the side of his head.

They lifted his left eyelid, shined a light, then let it close. They did the same with the right.

"Aaaaaah," Dad groaned.

"Dad!" I cried. "Mom! He's waking up!" I moved forward. Every-thing was gonna be—

Mom held out a hand to stop me.

He hadn't woken up. He was hurting in his sleep.

I felt something brush up against my legs. Looking down, I saw a massive cat, all black with one white spot on its tail and another around its left eye. It rubbed up against one of Molly's legs next, then turned in a circle to rub her other one.

"Oh!" A tall, thin lady rushed over. It took me a minute, what with trying to keep track of what was happening to Dad, but I remembered she was one of those early campers who'd checked into the camp-ground yesterday.

The cat tried to scoot away through the legs of all the people watching my dad, but the lady was too fast. She scooped the cat up, even though it pushed at her with all four of its paws. Tossing her waist-long brown braid over her shoulder, she chided the cat.

"Naughty kitty. Bothering this nice family when they're waiting to see if this man is going to make it!"

Mom gasped, and stiffened beside me.

"Make it?" Molly looked up at me, then asked Mom, "What's Daddy gonna make?"

I glared at the lady. "Dad's just knocked out!"

The lady's eyes blinked quickly several times. "Of course. Yes. I didn't mean . . . well . . . I'm sorry."

Officer Wyatt stepped up to Mom. When had he gotten here?

"Joan?" he asked. "What happened? For the record."

Mom put the back of her hand over her mouth and nodded at me, in a go-ahead kind of way.

I squared my shoulders, not looking at Mom, afraid of the disappointment I'd see.

"It's my f-f-fault."

"Your fault?" The officer tipped his head until our eyes met. "How?"

"Cooper?" Mom looked confused.

"I was late," I explained. "Dad told me to get his toolbox from the shed at the water tower and to come right back. But I didn't. I stopped first . . . and he called me on the radio, so I came back and . . . then . . . the tree was falling and Dad pushed me out of the way and—"

The words were in my mind, but they weren't coming out of my mouth the way I wanted them to. My throat clogged up. My eyes watered.

Officer Wyatt gave me a sympathetic look. "Where did you stop?"

"At my trail cam. I was only gonna be a minute, I swear. But then the fox kits came out of their den and—"

"Foxes!" The cat lady hugged her cat so tightly it pushed and struggled to get loose. "Den?" She looked from side to side, like the kits were hiding in the bushes, ready to pounce. As if! Like they'd stay anywhere near a loud-voiced lady and her crazy, clawing cat. "Foxes eat cats!"

"It's all my fault." I hung my head. "If I'd been here—"

"I don't—" began the officer.

"Oh, Cooper!" Mom cried. "You can't—"

Dad moaned again. And again. Hope rose in me, and I tried to peek around the EMT kneeling next to him, but all I could see was Dad's feet moving. When the EMT reached over into his emergency box, I finally got a good look. In spite of the white collar around his neck and the blue straps holding him down on the blue board, Dad struggled. The EMT said something, patting his shoulder, before searching the crowd with his eyes. Seeing me, he waved me over.

I took one step forward, not sure what the guy wanted. Had Dad told him how careless I'd been? Was I in trouble?

He waved some more. "Come on," the EMT coaxed.

I walked to him. His nod gave me the permission I was looking for. I knelt next to Dad. He looked awfully white. His right eye was swollen shut, a purple bruise around it. The other eye was watery, and focused on me.

"Coop——" he coughed. His good hand fluttered across the ground toward me and I grabbed it.

"Are you . . . o-kay?" I asked.

He nodded and closed his eyes. I looked quickly at the EMT, but all his attention was on my dad.

"Jim? Don't close your eyes. I need you to answer a couple of questions."

Dad blinked over and over until he could keep his eyes open. I heard soft footsteps behind me, and looked back over my shoulder to see Mom and Molly looking down.

"Jim," the EMT continued. "What day is it?"

What day is it? What kind of question was that?

Dad's brows came together. He looked up at Mom, then me. "Wednesday?"

The EMT nodded, as if that was the right answer. Which it wasn't.

I blurted, "Dad always says he doesn't know what day it is——"

Mom shushed me, and Dad's eyes darted from person to person, confused-like.

The EMT took Dad's good wrist in his hand, put two fingers on a vein, and looked at his watch. "Who's the president?" He sounded like he was asking Dad for directions to the lake.

My stomach got all twisted. *Barack Obama, Barack Obama,* I chanted in my head. *C'mon, Dad.*

Dad's face brightened. "George W. Bush."

I sucked in a breath. Something was wrong. Horribly wrong.

Still looking at his watch, taking Dad's pulse, the EMT said, "Good. Good. One last question. Do you remember the accident?"

Dad nodded very slowly. "I was cutting a tree. A crooked one. It was coming down, right in the spot I'd picked, when I saw . . . saw . . ."

"Go on," the EMT urged.

For the longest minute of my entire life, Dad and I stared at each other. His eyes were blank. Mine filled with tears.

"I saw him," Dad said, nodding my way. "The boy. He was late."

With every word, I felt as if the weight of the tree was hitting my shoulders again, pounding me into the ground.

"He's in shock," the EMT said, putting a hand on my arm. "Probably has a concussion, and if so, memory lapses are a sign, but in most cases, they're temporary. Don't worry."

Don't worry? Like, how do you do that, when your dad forgets your name?

Chapter 4

*Fox kits are born deaf and blind, and have fine,
gray woolly fur. It might take up to a week for
their eyes to open.*

Mom walked her gazillionth lap around the tiny waiting area since they'd taken Dad in to the examination room. With every other lap, she'd stop to look at a brochure with a big close-up picture of a cigarette across it, smoke rising off the white end. Why that brochure and not any of the others, I had no idea. No one in our family smoked.

Molly, who'd just finished a crying fit, sat on the floor at a coffee table, coloring a pony bright yellow. A grandmotherly nurse had given her the coloring book and a box of broken crayons to help calm her. Now, Molly hummed "You Are My Sunshine" under her breath. It was her favorite sing-with-Dad-before-bedtime song. She didn't fool me. The Squirt might look calm on the outside, but one wrong word, one wrong move, and she'd be screaming for Dad again in a heartbeat.

Now, I leaned up against a large, floor-to-ceiling window, looking out over a quick-moving, swollen river. My forehead resting on the cool glass, I watched a broken tree branch bob and duck as it moved downstream with the water. It neatly sideswiped a rock, twirled, then straightened.

"Are you okay?" With every lap, Mom stopped to ask this question. And like every other time, my throat started to close. My mind screamed *Do I look okay?* Instead, I nodded, not meeting her eyes.

She moved on to circle the room again, stopping to finger the smoking brochure.

The branch had gotten caught on a sapling growing sideways from a tiny island of brush in the middle of the river. Just beyond it was Great Falls, which wasn't really huge or anything. It was all the rocks and paths for the falling water that made it great. From here, I couldn't see the falls themselves. But they were there, just below where the water passed from my view.

Mom sat down on the coffee table next to Molly's coloring book. I let out the breath I didn't know I'd been holding. All that pacing was driving me crazy!

Suddenly, she stood, hands clasped together. The doctor had walked in.

"Mrs. Wilder?" he asked. At her nod, he smiled gently before looking down at his clipboard. When he cleared his throat, I glanced back out the window again at the river.

"Your husband is resting comfortably," he said. "He has a concussion, swelling in the brain, from the tree, or more likely a branch, hitting the right side of his head. His memory is returning and he'll have some headaches for a while. The frontal part of his brain—"

I tuned out all the big words filling the room as the doctor explained and Mom asked questions. The branch in the river had broken free and bobbed happily again, just traveling along, doing whatever a branch does, not knowing that everything in its world was about to change. I watched as it inched closer and closer to the edge of the falls, shot out into the air, hung there for a moment, kinda like, "Whoa! What just happened?," then *whoosh*. It dropped like a stone out of sight.

"We're also concerned about his arm." The doctor's voice had me looking at him again. "He's broken it pretty badly, just below the elbow, and we won't know exactly how badly until the swelling goes down and we can get an X-ray."

Molly leaned into Mom, looking back and forth between her and the doctor, eyes wide.

"Is Daddy coming home?" she asked.

The doctor hesitated. "No, I'm afraid not." At Molly's whimper, Mom gathered her close, and the doctor quickly added, "We need to watch him a little longer, okay? Just to be safe." To Mom, he said, "Our plan is to do an MRI tomorrow to look at his brain, and take X-rays of the arm. He's very drowsy, falling in and out of sleep, but he's been asking for all of you."

I wanted so badly to ask if he'd said my name. But I was afraid of the answer.

Molly put her hand in Mom's and practically pulled her after the doctor, as he walked toward the waiting-room door. My feet wouldn't move. I wanted to see Dad, but I didn't know if he wanted to see me. What if he pointed to the door and told me to leave? What if he—

Mom reached the door and looked behind her, frowning when she didn't see me.

"Cooper? Didn't you hear the doctor?"

I felt my eyes filling, as hers narrowed with worry.

"There you are!" Summer pushed sideways past the doctor and my mother. "I wanted to get here sooner, but I had to get my dad to drive me, and when he's deep in a project, it's hard to get him to stop." She crossed the room to stand beside me. I looked to Mom, who looked to the doctor.

"I'm sorry, but it's family only," he said.

"Go ahead." Summer pushed me toward my mom. "I'll wait here."

I followed them down the hallway, my feet still feeling like bricks as we passed doctors and nurses hurrying this way and that.

The doctor turned right into a small room. He grabbed the end of a curtain, which hung from a track on the ceiling, and pushed it to one side. "Jim, look who I found!"

Mom and Molly went right up to the bed. But my legs felt like they were knee-deep in mud.

Dad's eyes slowly opened. I could see his arm was bandaged to hold it still, and the right side of his head, by the ear, was purple. Molly bent over at the waist to put her head on Dad's chest, and he put a hand on her back to hug her as he whispered something. She giggled.

His eyes met mine.

"Cooper," he said simply.

Tears in her eyes, Mom smiled at the two of us. Then she took Dad's hand and squeezed it. His eyes closed again.

"Your husband's very tired," the doctor said, "and he needs his rest. But you can sit with him until visiting hours are over." He looked up at the clock on the wall. "You have an hour."

"Thank you," Mom said. "We'd like that." The doctor started to leave, but she asked, "How long will he be—" She waved a hand over him, then swiped tears from her cheeks.

Putting the clipboard under one arm, the doctor folded both arms in front of him.

"It's hard to tell this soon, but he'll probably be here for a day or two, and then he won't be able to return to work—as he knows it—for a couple of weeks."

A couple of weeks! But the camp! We open in a few days. How?

My mind raced with questions, but there were no answers, because the person with all the answers lay in the bed. The bed I'd put him in.

Suddenly, the room seemed too small. The walls were closing in. I had to go. I had to think. Clearing my throat first so my voice wouldn't crack, I said, "Summer's all alone—" I expected Mom to argue, but she just said, "Go ahead; he's sleeping. I'll send Molly to get you if he wakes up."

I backed out of the room, but at the door, I stopped. Mom now sat on the edge of Dad's bed. Molly lay beside him.

I'm so sorry, Dad, I thought. *I'll make it right. I'll get the camp-ground open. I'll have your back this time.*

I promise.

In the waiting room, I found Summer sitting on her hands in a chair, swinging her feet, and watching the giant television up on the wall, where the Red Sox were beating the Yankees. I sat beside her and she smiled at me. "How is he?"

"Sleeping," I said.

She nodded, and went back to watching the game. I breathed a huge sigh of relief that she didn't ask a million questions about Dad. She just . . . was there.

When I first met Summer, that day she and her father had moved into the old Wentworth house, I'd thought she was a girl. Well, of course, she is a girl. But I'd thought she was a girly girl. One who would worry about her blonde hair getting wet in the rain and her shoes black with mud from the trail. So I kinda ignored her. Only she wouldn't let me.

Last January, she'd cornered me in homeroom to ask for the hundredth time if I wanted to hang out. And I'd told her for the hundred and first time that I was too busy.

"Fine. I just thought you'd want to know about the perfect fishing spot," she'd said, tipping her head to one side, eyes daring me.

I'd laughed out loud. "You've only lived on the lake a couple weeks—"

"Months."

"Okay, months. How do you know the perfect spot?"

She'd raised her chin and flipped her ponytail in annoyance.

" 'Cause I caught three largemouth bass yesterday. And one the day before that."

"No way," I protested.

Summer held out her phone, and my so-called school friends gathered around as she scrolled through the photos.

"Where?" I asked.

"Uh-uh." Her ponytail swung from side to side again. "First, a bet. If I outfish you in *my* perfect spot, you have to stand up in front of the class and tell them so."

There was no way she'd win. "Sure. I'll take that bet."

Cooper and Packrat: Mystery of the Missing Fox

When she'd led me to a spot over the ice, just off the shoreline of the loons' nesting island, I'd known I was in trouble. This was Roy's favorite summer fishing spot, so it had to be a good one. Summer and I had made a hole in the ice and fished under the watchful eye of an eagle basking in the noon sunlight.

And she'd outfished me.

Her largest was a two-pound bass. Mine was a sunfish, which I threw out on the ice for the eagle, out of habit. Slapping my mittens together and shuffling from foot to foot from the cold, I remembered how I'd been trying to think up a way to gracefully ditch her and head for home, when suddenly, an adult eagle swooped down onto the ice.

Summer hadn't screamed. She hadn't shooed it away.

Her eyes had gotten bright and huge. She'd breathed one word. *Cooooooool.*

The eagle tilted its head to stare at us with one golden eye. It walked across the ice, talons scraping and gouging as it did, to peck at the flopping fish once, twice, before snatching it in a talon and flying away.

Summer had hopped up and down in excitement.

"Did you see that? Did you know it was going to do that?"

We'd talked—well, she'd asked a thousand questions, and I'd talked. Turns out she's a frog freak, and loves kayaking and eagles and hiking. Even geocaching.

Right then and there, I'd known two things: One, Summer was gonna be a cool friend to have; and two, I'd be letting everyone in homeroom know that I'd been outfished by a girl.

Chapter 5

Foxes communicate with one another through calls,
facial expressions, and scent marking.

The store had only been open for ten minutes the next morning, when Stacey, Packrat's mom, came sailing through the door.

"Joan! We got here as fast as we could!"

For a second, I thought Stacey was going to hop over the registration counter in her rush to hug my mom.

"Hey," Packrat said. He came in a little slower, hands in two of the many pockets of the long, tan trench coat he always wore, except when swimming. "Sorry to hear about your dad."

I smiled a little. "Thanks." I buried my own hands in the pockets of my jeans as Stacey held Mom. Tears fell from my mom's eyes for the hundredth time since yesterday.

And I'd put them there.

"Mom got me out of school." Packrat nodded toward the two of them, doing their hugging and crying thing. "She talked to my teachers and the principal last night. I got my homework. She made up lesson plans for her substitute teacher, and we drove straight down. I'm here for the week!" He grinned, but as fast as it appeared, it disappeared. "Stinks how it happened, though."

I gave him a nod. This was the best news I'd had in twenty-four hours. "Thanks," I said simply.

Mom wiped away her tears with the back of her hand.

"What am I going to do? Thanks to my bright idea," she said sarcastically, "we open in less than a week. Cameras are scheduled to roll for the *Camping with the Kings* show the day after that. I don't care if the campers show up and the place isn't perfectly perfect. But the King family? What will they think?"

"So cancel!" Stacey cried. "They have to understand; your husband's been seriously hurt!"

Mom shook her head. "I checked the contract. This is a reality show, not some fluff piece. His being hurt will actually make it more interesting." She sighed. "There's so much to do! Sites raked, roads cleaned up, flowers planted, water turned on, cabins and bathrooms super-cleaned, grading the driveway, stocking the store, boats to the lake—and that's just a few of the things on the list! I'll never finish them all by myself. And I need to be at the hospital—"

"I can help!" I cried, rushing to the counter. "I know how!"

When she gave me a sad Cooper-you-don't-really-know-what-you're-saying look, I slapped both hands, palms down, on the countertop and leaned into it. "I do! I've watched Dad a ton of times."

"Cooper," Mom sighed. "You have school next week."

I felt Packrat's finger poke my back, urging me on. I lifted my chin toward Stacey. "*She's* letting Packrat stay out of school; why can't I? To help you?" I quickly added.

Molly came out of the storage room. "No school, no school, no school!" She did a little twirl, showing off her purple dress, green tights, and yellow puddle jumpers. Mom had been too tired to argue over Molly's choice of clothes this morning.

"Molly!" Stacey hugged her. "You look awfully pretty today!"

"We're going to see Daddy." Molly twirled again. "These are his favorite colors."

"We'll go," Mom said, "right after lunch, as soon as we get a few things done."

Stacey took off her coat and flung it over a stool. "Don't forget me. I'm here to help. Show me what has to be done. We'll get you out of here in no time."

Mom's face brightened. "Jim's scheduled for tests this morning, and I'd love to go back after lunch."

HAH HAH, HAH, Hah!

We all turned toward the weird laughing sound. A really thin guy, not too short, not too tall, let the screen door shut behind him. My mouth dropped to the floor. Not because of his limping way of walking, but because he had the biggest, blackest raven I'd ever seen, on his shoulder.

The raven tipped its head to the side, then threw back its shoulders and opened its beak so wide, we could see the pink inside. *HAH, HAH, HAH!* it cawed again.

Packrat raised his eyebrows. Mom's mouth opened and closed, and I knew she was trying to find a nice, customer-comes-first way of asking if he'd seen the big red-and-white sign outside the store's door that said NO PETS ALLOWED. She always made it a big deal when I brought my three-legged frog Oscar in, because of sanitary laws or something. So I folded my arms and waited for the storm to hit.

Mom's eyes darted back and forth between the raven and the man.

"I . . . umm . . . you can't . . ." Then in a rush she blurted, "Pets aren't allowed."

"I'm sorry," the guy laughed, exactly as the raven had. "Didn't realize you were open. When I pulled in last night, no one was here to check me in. Honestly, I almost turned around and left because the place doesn't look anywhere near ready." He laughed again, and I took my eyes off the raven long enough to frown at him. What was so funny about that?

"But then a nice woman, walkin' with her cat, pointed to Maine Street. She said there were some frost-free-type water hookups for early birds like me and Bo, here. So, I took site number ten. Hope that's okay." The man nodded once. "Name's Vern, by the way."

Stacey's eyes flashed in annoyance as she waved him over to the registration counter. I wasn't sure if it was because the guy didn't take Bo back outside, or because he almost seemed like he was making fun of the fact that the place didn't look ready to open.

"We had an emergency yesterday, Vern, but I can take care of you now," she said curtly.

The man's smile turned into a more serious look. "I heard about it this morning, but can I make a suggestion? You should have put up a sign or something. I thought at first the whole campground was closed. And after I was told it wasn't, I didn't know which sites had electric or sewer. If it wasn't for the woman—"

"I'm sorry—" Mom began, but I cut *her* off.

"Yeah. We shoulda told the ambulance driver to wait ten minutes while we put up a sign for the one guy with the raven who might pull off the road." No one was gonna blame my mom, not when she hadn't done anything wrong. "Shoulda just left my dad lying on a stretcher, not knowing his own name—"

"Cooper! Enough!" Mom's eyes silently sent me a no-more-out-of-you look. To the man, she said, "I'm sorry. What my son is trying to say is that there wasn't—"

"Time," the man finished for her. He rubbed the back of his neck with his hand. "I'm sorry. I didn't realize it was your own husband who'd been hurt. I hope he's okay?"

Roy sauntered in the front door. "Hey, guys! I'm here!" He slapped a hand on my shoulder and gave Packrat a hey-there grin. I knew the minute he spied Bo, 'cause his mouth formed a round O. "Whoa!" he whispered, moving closer and putting his arm out in invitation. Bo looked at him and flapped his wings, but didn't leave the man's shoulder.

"Give him time," the man said, laughing once more. The raven joined him, calling *HAH, HAH, HAH, Hah!* It sounded like a bad recording of its owner, which had all of us smiling. Stacey gave the man the paperwork he needed to sign in order to stay as Mom came over to us. Apparently, the no-pets rule didn't apply to adorable ravens and their happy owners like it did for sons and their frogs.

Mom gave Roy a quick hug, which had Roy rolling his eyes in my direction. But he smiled, too. Still tight in her hug, he talked over her shoulder to us.

"When I heard Packrat was coming for the week, I convinced my mom to let me come, too. Help you guys get this place open." To Packrat, he added, "Hey, can I stay in your camper with you? Mom and Dad didn't want to open theirs up yet. Said it was too early. If it's okay with your mom, then they'll head back home."

Packrat smiled. "No problem."

"I can't thank you enough," Mom said, releasing Roy to give Packrat a quick hug, too. "But like I told Cooper, I'm not sure how much we'll be able to do without Jim."

She sighed and stared out the window over my head, biting her bottom lip. I held my breath. I knew that look. She was thinking about it. When she squared her shoulders, I knew she'd made a decision.

"I'm going to call the hospital to check on your dad. They were doing a—what'd they call it?—an MRI. This morning, I think. And an X-ray on his arm, right?"

I nodded, my eyes on her while stepping aside to let Vern and his raven leave the office.

"Okay, then. In the meantime, I have a job for you: Could you take this back to Summer?" Mom grabbed a black sweatshirt from the end of the counter and passed it to me. I remembered how Summer had used it to cover Dad until the ambulance got there. "We'll go see Dad after lunch, and maybe he'll be ready to come home today. And if he isn't, well, we'll pick his brain to make a list of things we have to do to get open."

"Soooo?" I rocked from my heels to my toes and back again. She had to let me. I couldn't keep my promise if she didn't.

Mom pulled me in for a hug. Sheesh, she sure was huggy lately.

"E-mail your teachers to get your work." She let me go just enough to hold me at arm's length and look me in the eye. "But," she glanced at Roy and Packrat, too, "all of you must promise to hit the books every night." She looked back at me. "Especially you. Deal?"

"Deal!" I said. And this time I wasn't going to let her, or Dad, down.

Molly started skipping in circles around us, then up the grocery aisle. "No school, no school, no school!"

Mom gave a quick shake of her head. "Oh, no, not you, young lady. You'll be going."

Molly stopped to stare at Mom with her what-did-you-just-say-to-me look.

Roy and Packrat and I slipped out of the store as Molly began her meltdown.

Chapter 6

Female foxes will make one or more dens when they know they'll be having kits. If they make multiple dens, they'll use the extras if the first is discovered by enemies.

Normally, I wouldn't be boating at the end of April, 'cause Mom wouldn't have let me. When I'd asked in the past, she'd said, "I've heard one too many stories about people drowning after falling in the frigid water."

That's one thing about owning a campground: Everyone has a story to tell. My mom soaks them all up, and uses them on me as examples.

I'm not sure if she said okay this time because she was distracted with worry over getting the camp ready to open, or because she thought *I* needed to be distracted—which had to be why she'd given me this totally not-urgent task—or because we'd had so many weird-for-this-time-of-year 70- and 80-degree days in April. I honestly didn't care. This would be my first kayak paddle of the season, and it almost made me forget about Dad's accident, his stay in the hospital, and having to get the camp open.

Almost.

Our campground boats hadn't been brought to the lake yet. Since Roy's parents weren't staying the week, they hadn't brought their motorboat up from Portland for Roy (Portland was home to him, when he wasn't camping with us). And Packrat and his mom hadn't taken the time to load their canoe when they'd left Weld to come down. So that left us with only one option: lugging the campground kayaks from their storage spot in the rec hall all the way to the lake.

Lucky for me, I had a golf cart. Half an hour later, we'd managed to pile three of the kayaks on the back of it, but just barely, and only if

Roy and Packrat sat in the passenger seat, turned around, and held the one on top.

We pulled away from the rec hall, with me going as slow as I could over the dirt road, concentrating on keeping my friends and the kayaks on the cart.

I heard a short, sharp whistle from the campsites, and a minute later, a raven soared through the playground toward the sound.

"You know," I said, "if there's one thing I wish I could do, it's fly like a bird. Soaring, you know? Not, like, in a plane."

"Me, too!" Packrat looked up at the sky like he was imagining it.

"I've always wanted to zip-line," said Roy, with a heavy sigh.

"Zip-line?" Packrat and I said at the same time.

"I'm not surprised," I added, laughing. Of the three of us, Roy was the one who liked to go fast. In his boat. On his bike. On his feet.

"Yeah," he shrugged, "or hang-gliding. I figure those are the two closest things to having wings of my own."

Once we had the kayaks on the beach, with our paddles and life jackets, I looked out over the water, trying to ignore the picnic area that needed raking.

The sky was blue, blue, blue. The sunshine was warm, and the cool spring breezes pushed the surface of the water first one way, then the other.

I tightened the straps on my life jacket before putting my kayak half in, half out of the water. Storing Summer's sweatshirt in the hatch first, I then put the kayak all the way in the water and held it out as far as my arm could reach. Placing one foot as close to the water as I dared, I balanced on it while stretching to put the other in the floating kayak. If I did it right, neither sneaker would get wet. Not even the toes.

I'd just pushed off with my paddle when Roy glided up on my right, Packrat not far after him, on my left. And I smiled to have us all back together on the lake again. I liked winter and snowshoeing and sledding, but oh, how I'd missed this feeling of floating!

We paddled in silence for a couple of minutes, finding our rhythm. Left, right, left, right, the water making a gentle dripping sound with each stroke.

Roy cleared his throat. "So, how bad? Your dad, I mean."

I shot him a sideways glance, only to find he wasn't looking at me, but at the end of his paddle.

"Bad," I said softly.

Packrat nodded. "That's what my mom said. Concussion, and broken arm?"

"But he'll be okay? Right?" If I hadn't known better, I would have thought someone new had joined us, because I didn't recognize the small, shy-like voice that came from Roy.

"Yeah. He should be home today or tomorrow."

"What happened?" Packrat asked. When I hesitated, he held up his hands, paddle still in them. "You don't have to tell us—"

I sighed. "Dad was cutting a tree. I wasn't there yet, but when I showed up, I ended up in its falling path. He ran over to push me out of the way and it fell on him instead."

"Whoa." Roy seemed to consider it for a minute. "So, like, what happened to his Rule of Two?"

"I was late. Coming back from—"

"And he started without you?" Roy's face got all funny, twisted. Kind of like he wanted to blow up, but couldn't decide who to blow up at. "Why were you late? Cutting trees is a dangerous business. Your dad always, always says—"

"I know!" I shouted. "But he coulda waited!"

"He *should* have waited." Packrat sent me a worried look, and then a sharp one to Roy. "It's his rule, after all."

Packrat only said what I'd been thinking since yesterday. But it didn't make me feel any better. And it didn't take away the guilt.

"Sorry," Roy said. "I'm just, you know, thinking about him."

"We all are," Packrat added. "So where *were* you coming from?" Packrat was soooo obviously trying to change the subject.

"I was supposed to get Dad's toolbox out of the shed up at the water tower."

Roy's shoulders and face relaxed. "Love that place."

"But I thought I'd stop at this den I found, and check on the trail camera I left there—"

"Big den or little one?" Packrat asked.

"Little. And suddenly, there were fox kits looking out at us! So I kinda started to watch them and forgot the time—"

Packrat grinned at me. "Us? Molly finally got you to take her on a wildlife watch?"

"No. Summer. We—"

Packrat stopped, his paddle raised. "She wildlife-watches with you?"

"Well, yeah."

The only sound I heard next was our paddles pulling through the water, rising, dripping water back into the lake, then sliding back into the lake again. I looked at Roy and he shrugged in a don't-ask-me kind of way. Packrat's face and voice were still Packrat-ish. But there was something there, just under the surface. He and Roy had only met Summer twice, when they'd come to visit over Christmas vacation week, right after Summer and I had first ice-fished together, and then again over February vacation. Both times she'd hung out with us, I'd noticed two things: One, Packrat hadn't talked unless someone said something to him; and two, he hadn't smiled much either. But he never once said he didn't want to hang out with her. I'd just figured he was shy.

Now, I wasn't so sure.

Roy pointed off to the right. Two adult loons were gliding together over by Ant Island. The water was so calm, their black-and-white markings reflected perfectly on the water's surface. One dove silently, barely leaving a ripple. The other put its head in the water, as if searching for the first; then it, too, dove. They both surfaced, one after the other, and greeted each other with head-bobbing and by swimming in circles.

Looked like we had our loon pair for the summer.

We pulled our kayaks up on Summer's little beach. She must have seen us coming, because she met us down by the water. She sure as heck didn't hear us paddling over, because old rock music was pouring out of her house.

"Led Zeppelin," she said with a sigh, pulling my kayak onto shore. "Dad's starting a new piece."

I got out of my kayak and opened the compartment. "I brought your sweatshirt."

Summer took it from me, opened it wide to look at it, then threw it over her shoulder.

"Thanks! You guys want a drink?"

"Sure!" I said, leading the way to walk up the small hill, and then the steps to her front porch. I reached for the door handle, but she squeezed past me to block my way. Pointing to three red Adirondack chairs, she said firmly, "Wait here," before slipping through her front door. We heard a click.

Packrat peeked in the windows. "What? We don't get invited in?"

Roy looked at the bottom of his boots. "It's not like I was gonna track in mud or anything."

I shrugged my shoulders. "She never lets me in. But when I see her dad at our place, he always says, 'Come and visit sometime!' "

Packrat frowned. "Maybe she's afraid we'll see something."

"Like what?" I asked. "Her dad's an artist."

The three of us leaned against the porch railing, staring at the front of the house. Roy folded his arms and grinned. "Maybe he paints."

Packrat threw his hands in the air. "Nothing weird about that! Why be so rude?"

Roy smirked. "Maybe he paints people with no clothes on."

Packrat and I burst out laughing. That would be a good reason, but I still didn't think that was it.

"Maybe it's just what Summer is always telling me," I suggested. "She says he doesn't like a bunch of people around when he's working. It might distract him or something."

Packrat got closer, his voice went low. "Maybe it's something like repainting already-famous stuff and selling it illegally."

"C'mon, Packrat," I pleaded. "I doubt it's anything like that."

A loud, long shriek rang out, echoing across the lake. We stepped off the porch and walked into Summer's yard to get a closer look at the nesting eagles, who were high in a tree nearby. One of the white-headed adults stood on the nest's edge, wings spread wide. It looked down at the water where the loon pair was diving and swimming. The other eagle adult flew in to land on a nearby tree, and began hollering with the first. I never did understand why those loons freaked out the eagles. It wasn't as if they could get to the eagles' nest and hurt their eaglets, the way the eagle could snatch one of the loon chicks in the blink of an eye.

"I guess the eggs haven't hatched yet," I said, watching as one of the adults walked down into the nest and rocked back and forth, until it sat so low, only the tip of its head could be seen over the side. "I told Summer to call as soon as both of them are standing up on the edge."

"I wonder how many chicks we'll have this year," Packrat said.

"It'd be cool to have quadruplets again!" Roy grinned up at the nest, no doubt remembering our adventure last summer.

That would be cool, I thought. But it'd be even rarer than having them in the first place.

The front door slammed and Summer practically jumped down her front steps. She looked wildly around until she found us.

"We gotta go back to your place!" she cried, pulling her sweatshirt over her head.

"But—" I began.

"Warden Kate called! There's trouble near the fox den!" She ran down the bank toward her dock and kayak. Packrat, Roy, and I were right behind her.

Chapter 7

A female fox is called a vixen. A male fox is called a dog.

That was the longest kayak ride and hike to the den, ever. Summer must have asked a hundred times what I thought could be wrong. Had something gotten the kits? The adults? The whole family?

Turns out, Warden Kate wasn't at the fox den. She was past it by a good five hundred feet or so, but I knew the area well. In the winter, I'd see fox prints here all the time. It wasn't too far off of our red-blazed hiking trail, either.

Through the bare trees and bushes, I saw the game warden up ahead, writing in her notebook. She wore her green uniform and a green warden cap on top of her short black hair. I looked all around, trying to see the emergency she'd called us for.

Packrat had grumbled under his breath all the way back from Summer's house, wondering why Warden Kate had called her and not us.

I rolled my eyes at him for the millionth time.

"I don't know! Maybe Mom told her we were over there."

In the middle of the forest, all lit up by the sun, was a large clearing with grass so thick, it almost looked like the kind of place in fairy tales, where you'd find a princess sleeping after having run through the woods to get away from bad guys. In the back right corner was a heap of branches and sticks, thrown there by someone a long time ago. Next to that lay a still, rusty-red form.

I rushed forward. Warden Kate put out an arm to stop me. I ducked under it.

The adult fox was on its side. Dropping to my knees, I put a hand toward it, then pulled it back.

"The mother?" I raised my eyes to Warden Kate, afraid of the answer. Afraid of what it would mean for the kits.

She shook her head. "This is a male."

The dad. This was the closest I'd ever been to a fox. The bright sunshine made its glossy fur shine. Eyes closed, it would have looked like it was sleeping, if not for the scratches and bite marks. And the fact that its left leg was caught in a foothold trap.

"Who found it?" Roy's voice was tight, angry, as he stood behind me.

"A hiker called it in." The warden knelt next to me. "At first glance, it looked like a hunter had set the trap and neglected to return and check on it, letting the fox die of starvation or dehydration. But once I looked closer, I saw that wasn't the case. Then, when I called Summer's—"

"House," Summer butted in. The warden and Summer shared a look, and Summer looked down at her hands. "Sorry, go ahead," she said.

"When I called, and Summer told me about the den, I wanted you all to come take a look."

"These marks . . ." Packrat pointed to the fox's legs and back.

"It got attacked?" I asked.

Roy bent down to where the snare trap clutched the fox's leg. He touched it with one finger, then let his finger trail down the little chain to the stake at the other end. "This is not hunting season."

"Even if it was," Packrat added, his eyes narrowed in anger, "it's illegal not to check a trap."

"Worse, it's illegal to put it on private property. My property!" I cried.

Roy nodded. "You got that right."

The warden pointed to the dirt around the trap. "See here? The ground is dry, and the fox prints are still fresh. I think this trap was set maybe two days ago, three at most."

"But the fox wouldn't have died in that short a time, would it?" Summer said softly.

"Something else got to it before the trapper." I pointed to a similar, but bigger, track. "Coyote."

The warden put a hand on my shoulder, then she stood. "I agree."

Packrat pulled a notebook and pencil from his coat and handed them to me. From another pocket he slid out a camera and began taking pictures. Warden Kate smiled at us. "You read my mind. Okay, let's put it all together now."

"Someone laid a trap here, next to the brush pile," Roy began, "probably because the fox had left tracks from hunting the mice and chipmunks that live in it."

Packrat got a close-up of the trap. "The fox stepped on the pan, releasing the spring, and"—he snapped his fingers—"was caught. But it was alive. You can see where it scrambled in circles, leaving prints in the dirt and tramping down the patches of grass."

I followed the larger prints around the outside edge of the clearing and across to the other side, Packrat trailing me with his camera.

"The coyote came in from here, and the fox was easy prey," I said, "since it had nowhere to go."

Summer kept looking between the three of us. "You three are like Shaggy, Fred, and Scooby."

The warden smiled at her. "I like to think of them more as the Three Musketeers, all for one, one for all. Protectors of wildlife."

Walking back to the trap, I looked to the warden for answers. "So what do we do about it? This is my property. We don't allow hunting because of it being a campground and all. The trail around the campground to the geocaches is close by; what if a camper had been walking here and gotten caught in it?"

"Or their dog?" Packrat said.

"Or their cat," I added, with raised eyebrows.

Summer gasped. "That's right! I forgot!"

"What? Cat?" Packrat and Roy asked at the same time.

"We have a fox-hating cat-owner lady in the campground," I quickly explained. "She was all freaked out when Dad got hurt, and I mentioned the den."

The warden frowned. "I admit it seems suspicious, but there's a big difference between protecting your cat and getting involved in illegal trapping."

"Can I take the trap off its leg?" Roy asked.

"Sure," Warden Kate said. "Just wear some—"

"Gloves," Packrat held up one black work glove triumphantly, like a trophy, then did a double take. He started going through his pockets again. "I know I had two. Where'd the other one go?"

"Summer?" the warden asked. "Can I talk to you for a minute? About the fox—"

"You want a statement, right?" Summer shot me a worried look. "About what I told you on the phone? Cooper and me seeing the kits?"

The warden tipped her head to one side and gave a slow nod.

Summer's eyes darted back to me. I nodded and shot her a nothing-to-worry-about smile.

Summer sent me back a grateful look before walking away with Warden Kate. When I looked back up, they were in the center of the clearing, talking together.

Packrat patted his pockets. "Hmm . . . I know I had it."

"What?"

"The other glove. I bet I dropped it when we were looking for coyote prints. I'll check it out."

As Packrat retraced his steps across the clearing, Roy asked, "Does it make you mad?"

"The trap? Yeah! They've no right putting it on my property," I said.

"No. Trapping. Does trapping make you mad?"

I hesitated. I never really knew how to answer that question. It was one of those subjects that could split a group sitting around a campfire as quickly as an ax splits a log. Me, I stood in the middle.

"No, I don't hate trapping if it's done right," I said. "We need it. To keep some wildlife populations under control, you know. To help feed

41

people. Or to relocate an animal. But this isn't trapping, it's poaching, for two reasons: It isn't fox-trapping season, and this isn't the trapper's land."

Roy nodded, his eyes not leaving the fox's face. "This guy didn't stand a chance against that coyote, though."

Packrat hurried back, a worried look on his face. He glanced back the way he'd come, and shook his head once. Tossing a pair of gloves at Roy and another pair to me, he muttered something under his breath.

"What?" I asked.

"What? Umm, nothing." He bent down over the fox as we disassembled the trap to put it into a large plastic bag for the warden.

I frowned at the back of his head and looked back. Summer stared in earnest at Warden Kate, waving her arms, almost like she was pleading. The warden looked like she was patiently trying to explain something to her. She put a hand on Summer's shoulder, in a calm-down-no-need-to-be-upset kind of way.

"Are they fighting?" I put a hand on the ground to stand up, thinking I could go over and fix whatever was going on. But Packrat tugged on my shirt to keep me down.

"Not exactly fighting."

I glanced back again, and Summer met my eyes for a second before ducking her head.

"All I heard—" Packrat paused. "All I heard was the warden saying, 'Ask your dad when you get home,' and Summer said something like 'My dad doesn't have—' "

"So?"

"So? Weird, right? Looks like we have two suspects now."

"Two?" I asked.

"Cat Lady and Summer's dad."

I frowned. "Summer's dad isn't a suspect. He lives across the lake. He's an artist."

Packrat shook his head. "Summer shushed the warden when I went over there. She didn't want me to hear that her dad is suspected of trapping."

I shook my head. "Now *you're* being weird. She's just giving her statement, Packrat."

"So why didn't the warden ask you for yours?"

"You two about done chatting?" Roy held the limp fox in his arms. "Let's get out of here."

I handed my notes back to Packrat, who stashed them in his pocket with the camera. I grabbed the bag and, as I stood, I heard him say, "I hope you're right, Cooper. But her dad is going in my Maybe column."

Chapter 8

Young kits first practice pouncing on insects, leaves, twigs, and their parents' tails. The parents will eventually bring back live mice for them to practice on. Learning to hunt on their own is a very important step in the kits' lives.

When we got back from the woods, and the warden had transported the fox to the biologists for research, Mom, Molly, and I went to see Dad at the hospital.

He sat up in bed and smiled broadly when he saw us in the doorway.

"Finally! Someone to talk to," he exclaimed.

Molly ran across the room and threw herself on his bed. Dad hugged her tight, even though he winced in pain when she leaned into his arm. I could see that the bruise along the side of his head had grown brighter. It was like a neon sign; you couldn't quite look away from it.

"Cooper, come here," Dad urged.

My feet itched to do as he asked, but it took Mom's gentle hand on my back, pressing me forward, to move me to his bedside.

"It looks worse than it is, buddy. And my headache is down to a dull roar."

"And your arm?" Mom asked.

Dad sighed. "Believe it or not, that's what's going to keep me from going home today." When Molly whimpered and put her head on his chest, Dad put his hand on her hair. His eyes met mine. "The break is a bad one. They have to put a pin in it. That means surgery—"

"Surgery!" Mom moved closer to the bed. Molly practically crawled under the covers with him.

I took a small step back.

"They would have done it today, but the swelling is still too bad. And the surgeon is away at a conference or something." Dad ran a hand through his hair, the tubes and wires attached to it dangling with the movement. "Bottom line, they're keeping me here for another day or two. They'll do a second MRI. The surgery on the arm, then I can go home, but . . ." Dad's voice drifted off.

"But?" Mom asked quietly. Hesitantly.

"I've been warned that I can't work with heavy machinery. Light work only, for a while. I can't cut down trees, open the bathrooms, get the water on . . ."

Suddenly, Dad's happy-to-see-us face was lined in worry.

"Stacey can run the office while I tackle your chores," Mom suggested.

"You can't do it by yourself," Dad cautioned.

"We'll hire someone."

Dad shook his head. "We can't afford that."

"I'll get us ready," I said.

"Cooper, you can't—"

"I'm tired of everyone telling me what I can't do!" I cried. "Dad, I've watched you do these things a million times!"

Dad half-chuckled. "We've only owned the place a couple of years." He shifted in the hospital bed as he eyed me up and down. "But I do know what you mean. When I get home, maybe I can—"

"Not then, Dad, now. What can I do *now*?" I stepped closer to the bed, willing him to understand. "Please. I need to do something. Anything."

Dad was wattling, I could feel it. He just needed a little more convincing.

"Packrat and Roy are back. They're staying this week to help us get ready for Friday. For the *Camping with the Kings* show."

"Really?" Dad put a hand down next to his hip, on the hospital bed mattress, and pushed down to sit up a little straighter. His eyes brightened as they went from Mom to me. "I suppose it can't hurt to try, right? Got a paper and pencil?"

Molly sat up. "I want to help, too!"

Dad chuckled. "I'm sure we can come up with something," he said.

"Sooooo, I'm gonna get to stay home from school, too?" she asked, shooting Mom a sneaky grin.

Dad kissed the top of her head. "Sure, why not?"

"Jim!" Mom exclaimed, but for the first time since the accident, I saw smiling eye-talk flash between them. "I spent the whole morning telling her she couldn't!"

"Let the girl help. She needs to feel useful, as much as Cooper does."

No. Not as much as I did. Nowhere near as much.

When we got back to the campground late that afternoon, Mom called a meeting. Roy, Packrat, Stacey, and I gathered around a table with her in the coffee area, while Molly colored a get-well card for Dad. Between us was the list of things Dad said absolutely, positively had to be done in order to open the campground on May 1. Mom had also laid out a site map. Most of the campground was highlighted, except the section where Dad had gotten hurt.

"After looking at the list, I think, between all of us, we can do most of the things Dad mentioned," Mom said.

The front door opened and we heard footsteps running through the store.

"I'm here!" Summer cried, pulling up a chair between Packrat and me.

I slid my chair over to make room, but Packrat wasn't budging. I kicked him in the leg. He sighed heavily, then moved over so she could slide in.

Summer grinned at all of us. "My dad said I could take a couple days off from school, too!" she announced.

Mom smiled warmly at her. "Many hands make light work," she quoted. Pointing to the map, she got down to business.

"These are the sections of the park easiest to open up. And it's how many sites we'll need for opening weekend, for the reservations I've already taken, and for the motorhomes with the *Camping with the Kings* show. The most important thing to do will be—"

"Rake the sites?" I asked.

"That will be last," Mom said, "if we get them done at all. As much as I want the sites and recreation areas raked, flowers planted, and boats on the dock, so the campground looks pretty for the footage the cameras will take, that all has to come last." Mom took a deep breath, and continued, "Because if the water isn't on, the roads aren't cleared, and the bathrooms and rental cabins aren't open and clean, that would look far worse on the show. So those things come first. If there's time, we'll do the rest."

Stacey put her chin in her hand, elbow on the table. "Hmm . . . let me handle the office and taking reservations, okay? I know how to do that, but I don't know a hammer from a screwdriver. That should free you up to tackle some of these other jobs."

Mom gave her a grateful look before turning to me. "Your dad left instructions on how to turn the water on. He even drew a diagram of the wellhead, where the valves are and things like that. You know where that is, Coop?" Mom looked a little unsure. "No, wait. Why don't I send you boys to dust and wash down the rental cabins and I'll work on the well—"

"I know how," I interrupted, making sure to sound like I really did know all about turning the water on. I only kinda did, but anything was better than cleaning cabins.

Mom tapped her pencil on the map for a minute. "Okay, deal. First you turn the water on, then chlorinate the well and lines. This map is just for you. When it's time, you'll need it to see the direction you have to follow when you start opening the water spigots on each site, checking for leaks, and then letting the water flow through to clean out the lines and get rid of the chlorine." She took a deep breath. "Cooper, as I explain this out loud, it sounds like we're asking an awful lot of you."

"How hard can it be?" Roy said.

"Yeah," I agreed. "Really. It's just turning on water."

Mom and Stacey looked at each other with an aww-isn't-he-cute-he-wants-to-help look.

"I wish it were that simple, boys. But there's a certain way it has to be done."

Suddenly, a black feathered blur flew to the middle of the table, wings flapping, making the papers skitter across the table. Stacey

gasped, while Mom and Molly threw their hands over their heads. The rest of us slid back in our chairs as far as we could go.

"It's only Bo!" I said, as the raven calmly tucked his wings next to his sides. He tipped his head, giving us what seemed like a why-wasn't-I-invited look. He eyed each of us, until he saw Packrat. With a rolling walk, kind of like his owner's, he headed right for my friend and dropped a silver carabiner clip on the table by his hand.

"He likes ya." Vern's voice came from behind the chips rack.

I laughed. Of course Bo would like Packrat. Ravens like to pick up things and stash them away for later.

Vern limp-walked up to the table, putting one hand on the edge of it for balance.

"So sorry. He can't resist shiny things. The rack on your counter— it's way too tempting, I'm afraid."

Vern reached over Packrat to take the carabiner back, but Bo pecked his hand gently before sliding the clip closer to Packrat with his beak.

"Thanks!" Packrat said to Bo. "I'll pay you for it, Mrs. Wilder. I've never had a raven give me a present before."

I could tell Mom really didn't know what to do with all of this. She tucked a lock of hair behind her ear before asking Vern, "Can we help you?"

He smiled, "Yeah, I was lookin' to sign up for another night and I hope you don't mind, but I heard voices . . ." He cleared his throat. "And I didn't mean to eavesdrop, but I could use the work."

Mom stammered, "Well . . . thank you. But I . . . we . . . can't pay you."

Vern scratched his head, then looked at Bo as if he were silently asking a question. To us he said, "I need to stay for a while, on account of my seeing a knee specialist in Portland. The hotel I was staying at asked me to leave when they found out I had Bo."

Summer stared at his bum leg. "But how will you . . . work?"

"Summer!" Mom was horrified. I bumped Summer's shoulder with my own. She hung her head. "I didn't mean anything, I just—"

Vern laughed, Bo echoing him. "I can do anything, except maybe climb. This bum knee doesn't like to bend the way it's supposed to. What do ya say? I'll work to pay off my campsite, and do the things your boy here can't."

Bo squawked in agreement.

Mom's face looked hopeful. "I'd need to talk to my husband first."

"References," Stacey suggested.

"I can get ya those," Vern said. "I'll have 'em in the mornin'."

As Vern left the store whistling, Bo perched on his shoulder, Mom sat back in her chair with a happy sigh. Cupping her favorite coffee mug with two hands, the one with the loon picture on it, she exclaimed, "We just might pull this off!"

Chapter 9

Foxes have approximately twenty-eight sounds
for communicating, some for long distances
and some for short.

After we'd made a plan of what jobs had to be done in order for the campground to open by Friday, and when the store had cleared of people, Mom locked the front door for the night. I started picking up the coffee area and wiping down the tables. Summer helped by throwing out the napkins and straightening chairs. Packrat's mom went to shut down the computer and turn on the answering machine. Then Mom grabbed a broom and began sweeping.

Molly chose this moment to grumble. "I'm hungry!"

Mom looked at her watch, then the clock on the wall. "Is *that* the time? What was I thinking? I forgot all about feeding you." She poked Molly's stomach. "But you don't need to eat, right?"

Molly, the little drama queen, clutched her stomach and gave Mom a puppy dog look. " 'Course I do!"

Mom smiled, but it didn't quite reach her tired eyes. "Let me think." She swept the dirt pile into a dustpan and dumped it into the trash can. "Something easy."

"Macaroni and cheese!" Molly exclaimed.

I went into the grocery aisle. Holding up a blue-and-yellow box, I said, "Got it—"

Molly shook her head. "No! Dad's 'Mazing Macaroni!"

Mom's shoulders sagged. She bit her lip.

I glared at Molly. She stuck out her tongue.

Without saying a word, Mom put her broom and dustpan away. She lifted my sister up, setting her on the counter and looking her in the eye. In an instant, I knew that Molly could tell Mom would say no. And Molly would have a Molly Meltdown when she did.

And Summer was about to witness it all. Unless . . .

"Campfire?" I blurted, not exactly sure why it'd popped into my head.

Mom and Molly turned my way. Molly's eyes changed from blowup red to sparkly blue. "Campfire!" She rushed to give me a big hug around my waist.

Mom looked confused. "Campfire?"

Packrat and Roy gathered on either side of me.

"Hot dogs?" I was warming up to the idea.

Packrat opened the left side of his coat, pulling out some twelve-inch metal roasting sticks. Mom shook her head. "Those aren't long enough—" she started.

Packrat put a hand on each end and pulled them all the way out to three feet long.

Mom rolled her eyes and laughed out loud. "I should've known." To Summer, she added, "I fall for it every time."

Roy rubbed his hands together gleefully. "I haven't had hot dogs over the campfire since last fall!"

"I've never had hot dogs over the fire," Summer said shyly.

Mom smiled at me over Molly's head. She mouthed the words *Thank you* as the little brat bounced up and down.

I sighed. Molly was overtired. And she missed Dad. I really oughta give her more of a break.

Packrat's mom added chips and rolls. Packrat pulled marshmallows from another pocket, and just like that, there it was—a full course meal. Camping style.

"It feels odd, having a campfire without your father," Mom said, as she lit a small lantern on the wooden picnic table that held our supper supplies. She didn't sound sad, just matter-of-fact. "I can't remember him ever missing one. It really is his thing."

Packrat handed his roasting fork to me, which held three hot dogs side by side on two metal teeth, over the red-hot coals. Then he stood up to open his jacket. We all stopped what we were doing, to see what he was going to do.

"Hey!" He pointed at the hot dogs. "Don't burn 'em! Turn 'em!"

I grinned, and went back to slowly turning the hot dogs over the flames. Reaching into one of his many inner pockets, he pulled out a tablet. In the glow from the screen, I could see Packrat's concentration as he tapped a series of tabs. Suddenly, we heard, "Hello? Hello?"

"You're on FaceTime, Mr. W." Packrat grinned at the tablet. "Take the phone away from your ear. Look at it."

Packrat turned the tablet around, and Molly gasped in excitement. "Daddy!"

Dad looked back at us with a big goofy grin. "A campfire! Hey! What a surprise!"

Packrat handed the tablet to my mom.

"Oh, you hold it," she said.

"Can't. Cooper's gonna burn the hot dogs!"

He took back the roasting stick, pretend-muttering about how I liked them black like my marshmallows. Which I did. But I was the only one.

"Might as well drop them in the fire," he said.

"And I suppose you like to eat yours with ketchup, too," I teased.

"It's the only way!" Roy joined in.

"Not ketchup?" Summer asked. "Then what?"

"Mustard and relish," I said. "Ketchup is for fries."

Packrat gave me a little shove with one hand. I punched him in the arm.

"No pushing by the fire!" Mom reminded us.

I rolled my eyes. But we stopped.

Dad chuckled. "Just like being there in person."

I'd taken my first bite of juicy hot dog when Vern walked into the circle, Bo on his shoulder.

"Mind if I sit down?"

Mom said, "Please do."

Once he sat, she introduced him to Dad, which seemed a little weird, since he—or, really, the tablet—was now propped up in a chair. But Vern didn't even bat an eye.

"Where're you from?" Dad asked.

"Up north, just over the Canada line." Vern smiled when Bo squawked. "He always makes noise when I say—umm—my country's name."

"You say the surgery brought you here?" Mom asked.

"Well, the operation I need on this bum knee of mine is very special-ized," he explained, patting his left knee. "You have one of the few doc-tors on the Northeast coast who can do it, right in Portland. I'm waiting on my insurance to approve the visit. Without it, I can't get the surgery. Which is why I need to stick around for a bit, 'til it's all sorted out."

"Joan told me about your offer to help us get open. We sure appreciate it," Dad said.

I stared at the tablet with his image. Droopy eyes and a bruise that still shined. But the edges of his mouth curved upward tonight.

"Mmmmm!" Summer said, her eyes rolling upward, her mouth full of hot dog. "These are soooo good! Can I have another one, Packrat?"

"How'd you live this long without having a hot dog over a fire?" he grumbled, taking another hot dog off the table behind him.

"Wish I could have one of those hot dogs," Dad said. "Hospital food really stinks."

Packrat looked at the tablet for so long, I held my breath. But then he shook his head.

"Nope. Not even I can make that happen, Mr. W."

As we all laughed, Roy got up to bring back the bag of marshmal-lows. Molly threw her paper plate on the fire, then leaned into Mom, who kissed the top of her head and stroked her hair.

I saw Cat Lady walking down the street, her faithful black-and-white cat following behind like a dog. She hesitated outside the circle, but Mom called her in with a wave of her hand.

"I don't want to interrupt," she said.

"Not at all! Please join us," replied Mom. "Everyone, this is Mad-eline Nichols."

Cat Lady nodded to each of us as she chose the chair to the right of Vern. Bo got fidgety, flapping his wings and rocking from side to side.

I glanced down at the cat, who'd sat next to its owner's feet and was looking around regally.

Bo flew down to perch on the arm of his owner's chair. The cat glanced up at Bo once, licked a paw, then jumped up into Cat Lady's lap, where it turned around twice before curling up and settling down.

Bo tipped his head and stared.

The cat stared back.

"Cooper?" Dad's voice cut through my thoughts. "Put another log on the fire, would you?"

I got up to go to the woodshed, and brought back two big logs. I tossed one on the fire and we all paused to watch the sparks shoot up into the air, four feet high, then go out, one by one by one.

Maaaaaaaah!

The sharp, screeching call cut through the dark, quiet night. I jumped up from my chair. Roy dropped his roasting stick, the gooey marshmallows falling in the dirt at his feet. Molly and Mom sat straight up, trying to look beyond the darkness.

Cat Lady whispered, "Somebody's in trouble!"

"A woman screaming?" Roy stood, on alert.

"A little girl!" Packrat cried, patting the pockets of his coat. He pulled out a small flashlight. "Let's go!"

"No, wait—" Vern began, as Bo flew to a nearby branch. Even the cat sat up, one ear turned toward the woods.

"Listen!" I ordered.

Everyone went silent.

Maaaaaaaah!

It was closer now, moving through the woods.

"You know what it is?" Dad asked.

I shook my head. "But not a person," I said quietly, because I wanted to hear the sound if it came again. "An animal."

None of us made a sound as we waited. The fire crackled and clicked. A camper door slammed shut a few sites down. I began to relax. Roy picked up his roasting stick. He slid off the now-dirty marshmallows and tossed them into the fire. He slid on two more, and hung them over the shimmering red coals. The hissing of the hot wood lulled me, as I started planning in my mind how I would go into the wellhead tomorrow, getting the water on and—

MAAAAAAAAH!

That sound again! Right behind me! I jumped up and turned, coming face to face with a cringing Summer. Holding up her phone, she said meekly, "Sorry! That was louder than I thought. I recognized it, the sound. But I didn't want to be wrong, so I looked it up, and I was right! It's the fox call for—"

"A fox!" Cat Lady scooped the cat up in her arms. It scrambled and pushed at her with its paws. Breaking free, it leapt off the chair, walked over to the picnic table, and jumped up on it, sitting with a harrumph.

"Yes," Summer explained. "It's the call for distress."

I sighed. "Oh, that makes sense."

"What do you mean?" Mom asked.

"A hiker found the male fox in a trap today," Roy said, sitting back down to keep turning his marshmallow over the fire.

At her gasp, I looked at the woman across the circle from me. In the dark, with the orange glow dancing across her face, it was hard to read it.

"Well, I'm glad somebody has some sense," she said. "We don't need foxes around here."

"Yeah, we do!" I cried. "Foxes keep the rat, mouse, rabbit, and chipmunk populations in check. Some of the plant life, too."

"Ya know . . . ," said Roy slowly. We all turned to him as he touched his marshmallow with his thumb and pointer finger, once, twice, then slowly pulled the ooey, gooey, sticky mess off to pop it in his mouth. One cheek popped out, he continued, with his mouth full, ". . . with no foxes, we'd be overrun with rats."

"Oh, boy," Packrat chimed in. "Then they'd be going in everyone's trailers, looking for shelter and food."

Mom shot Dad a look, almost like she was asking him to step in to the conversation. Dad just raised an eyebrow and smiled.

I felt a smile on my face, too, so I quickly tipped my head down and got busy poking the fire.

Maaaaaaaah! The call was going farther away.

"Harrumph!" Cat Lady sat back in her chair and folded her arms. To Dad, she spoke overly loud, like he'd have a hard time hearing her through the tablet. "Just what are you going to do about those foxes?"

"Do?" he asked.

I stood up, to stare down at her.

"What do you mean, do? They have kits—a den! They live here, too. There's nothing *to* do!"

Vern asked, "Kits? Interesting."

The lady glanced at me, but turned right back to Dad like I was invisible or something.

"A whole family of them then? Are you going to trap them? Catch them? Bait them? How are you going to get rid of them?"

A hot ball formed in my stomach. It started rising, rising, rising, like the sparks from the campfire. My face felt flushed. My mouth twitched with all the un-customer-servicey words I wanted to say, but knew I couldn't.

"It's nature!" Mom said gently to Mrs. Nichols, with an if-you-can't-say-something-nice-then-don't-say-anything-at-all look of warning to me. "We don't *do* anything about it unless they are, say, denning under the workshop."

"But they could come after my cats!"

Roy had frozen midway to putting another marshmallow on his roasting stick.

"Cats? With an 's'?" he asked.

"Of course! I can't leave them back at home alone while I camp here."

I knew I'd regret knowing, but I had to ask, "How many?"

"Four." She held up a hand, four fingers spread wide as she pointed to them in turn. "Fluffy, Frisky, Darling, and, of course, Fred."

All together as one, we said, "Fred?"

Cat Lady shrugged. "That was the name on the adoption papers, when I picked up the little darling last week. Doesn't answer to anything else. And I tried. Sugar. Petunia."

"Well, duh!" Summer threw her hand in the air. "If he's a guy cat, he isn't going to come to those girly-girl names." She gave me a what-is-this-lady's-problem look.

"I like all their names," Molly said, yawning.

"You don't understand, I didn't . . . Oh, never mind. It doesn't matter. Bottom line, I need to protect my cats. Can't you see? Tell me where those foxes are!" she pleaded.

"And then what, Madeline?" Vern had been silent this whole time, but his soft, even voice threw a blanket on the smoldering argument.

She sighed sadly. "I don't know. I just want to protect my cats."

I knew my voice was rising, but I couldn't stop the words from pouring out.

"They won't go after your cats, if you keep them close. In fact, put 'em on leashes if you're that worried!"

"Leash my cats!" Cat Lady stood up, putting a hand to her throat like I'd just told her to wear one, too. "But they're natural hunters. They like to roam!"

"So do foxes. And they were here first," Packrat said.

"The boy has a point," Vern said. "And there's more to worry about than foxes around here, you know."

I swear I heard Dad laugh quietly from the tablet in the chair. Mom frowned his way.

"Like . . . what?" Cat Lady asked.

"Fishers," Packrat said.

"Coyotes," I added.

"Eagles," Roy chipped in.

We all turned to Summer. She looked up thoughtfully. "Loose dogs."

Cat Lady harrumphed again. "Let's go, Fred," she said, and stalked off, not even looking back to see if her little darling followed.

"Leashes?" Roy scoffed. "Really?"

I shrugged. "I've seen them. Better safe than sorry."

"You all know your wildlife," Vern stood. "But you know foxes don't usually take cats unless food is scarce, right? Especially not large ones like hers."

"I know. But she"—I nodded toward Cat Lady's retreating figure—"won't believe me."

Vern nodded. "No. She probably won't." His gaze touched on us all as he said, "So, nine tomorrow morning? Meeting at the office?" We all nodded.

Suddenly, Cat Lady was back, calling to her cat. "Fred! I thought you were right behind me!"

With all the commotion, I'd forgotten about the pets. Looking beyond the campfire, I saw Fred and Bo sitting side by side on the picnic table. No hissing. No cawing. Just hanging out.

I sighed. Why can't humans and nature be that way?

Chapter 10

Red foxes can swim, but they don't like to. They travel mostly on land, and prefer well-worn trails through the woods and fields.

When Dad's eyes got droopy, Mom urged him to go and rest. Dad thanked Packrat again for bringing him into the fire circle.

"No medicine they've given me here has helped half as much as hanging out at the campfire with all of you," he said, before saying good night.

Summer looked at her phone. "My dad should be here soon."

Molly was curled up on her side on the bench, her head in Mom's lap. Mom played with Molly's hair as she looked at Summer. "You know, I don't think I've ever heard what your father does. For work."

I sat straight up in my chair. Packrat stopped poking the fire, and Roy sat perfectly still. Usually, I groan at Mom and beg her to stop when she asks my friends a ton of wanna-get-to-know-you-better questions. But not tonight. Because we all wanted to know the answer.

Summer gave me a helpless look over the campfire. I smiled back at her.

"He, umm, works from home," she finally answered.

"That must be nice," Mom said. "To always have him there, I mean. Does he have an office in town, too?"

"Umm, nooooo."

Mom tipped her head to one side. "He's a salesman?"

"He's a . . . he's an artist."

Suddenly, Summer couldn't sit still. She sat on her hands, then clasped them in her lap.

"Really?" Mom's face, lit by the campfire, held a gentle smile. "What medium does he work with? Painting? Pottery? Oh, I used to love pottery; I haven't done it in years."

Summer pulled her ponytail over her shoulder into the front. She looked down at her hands as they separated and then smoothed the ends of it. "Oh, it's weird stuff. Really artsy, and you know, some people, they don't get it."

The loons wailed, giving Summer's explanation a hint of sadness.

"Oh, honey," Mom said, "don't let what other people think keep you from seeing the art form. There's beauty in all art. All of it. In Impressionism. Surrealism. Pop Art. Realism."

Summer tensed for a second. Then she relaxed. Her hands stopped poking at her ponytail. She smiled. "Yes, that's what he does. Realism."

Realism. Really? Somehow, I didn't think that's what "it" was. Her dad didn't seem like the paint-it-the-way-it-is type. No way Mom would buy that.

Molly sat up and yawned. Mom stood, silently urging her onto unsteady feet, all the while still talking to Summer.

"I'm sure he does amazing work. I'd love to see it sometime."

Wait! What? Mom wasn't giving up that easy, was she?

Mom gently steered Molly home by the shoulders, in spite of the fact she protested all the way.

"I don' wanna go—" Molly yawned and wiped her eyes with the back of her hand.

"Tomorrow's another day, little girl." Mom yawned along with her. "Half an hour more, boys," she called back. "We have to get an early start tomorrow."

I poked the fire once, twice, moving the embers around, letting them burn.

I couldn't believe Mom had bought Summer's story. Packrat and Summer and Roy had moved to stand around the fire ring with me. Roy put his hands over it, trying to soak up the last of the rising hot air.

"Do you think the mother fox was calling for the male?" he asked.

"Or was it a kit, calling for its dad?" Summer wondered.

"I don't think the kits can make that sound yet," I said, poking the fire again, making it hiss and pop. "Must have been the female."

"Hey!" Summer asked, "Did you ever look at the memory card? The one you got when we checked the kits the day your dad—"

I slapped my hand to my forehead. "I totally forgot!"

I dug in the pocket of my sweatshirt, the same one I'd been wearing that day. Finding it in the very bottom crevice, I pulled it out. Packrat took it from me to put it in his camera. He pushed a couple of buttons and held it out to show a video of five kits scrambling out of the hole after their mother, who was leaving the den. The next video showed an adult fox sitting next to the den, tail swinging back and forth while two of the kits wrestled. Eventually, they tumbled one over the other down the bank as the mother fox looked on.

"Wow!" Packrat said. "Your trail cam is in a great spot!"

The next video showed the mother sitting in the same spot. When a kit scurried up the little hill, she pounced so her front paws landed right in front of it, almost like she was telling her kit, "Hey! What'd I say about wandering too far away!" The kit got low to the ground and looked up at her in a sorry kind of way.

"Nothing suspicious on here," I said, as we watched the last video of tumbling kits. "At least we know the poacher didn't come near the den."

Roy pointed his now-empty roasting stick toward Packrat's camera. "Anyone tries to mess with it, though, you'll have proof."

"I'm so glad Cooper and I found the kits!" Summer said softly.

Packrat quickly said, "Did you guys know that newborn kits can't stay warm on their own? And the mom has to be, like, their blanket every minute for the first two to three days? The male feeds her, and the kits drink her milk."

Summer snorted. "Everyone knows that. More interesting is how foxes swallow their food whole—fur, bones, and all."

Roy yawned. Then Summer, too. Feeling a yawn well up at the back of my throat, I said, "Pass the water hose."

Packrat pulled out his mini flashlight to find and uncoil the water hose from a hook on a nearby tree. Before walking back, he kinked the hose and turned the water on.

I moved to one side so he could drag the hose right over and turn it on the fire. Then he began poking the coals, sliding them apart, playing more than anything else.

Suddenly, I heard water splashing, but it wasn't on the fire.

"Hey!" Summer cried, jumping back as the stream of water passed over her sneakers on its way to the fire ring. "Watch it!"

"Sorry," Packrat said, kinking up the hose again and tightening his fist around it. His voice sounded anything but sorry.

Summer raised one foot to shake it, then the other. "Why'd you do that?"

"It wasn't like I did it on purpose!" Packrat insisted. "Geez!"

"Sure, you didn't!"

"I didn't! The hose unkinked by accident." He raised his fist, the one holding the hose, and we all took a step back. "Happens all the time! Tell her, Cooper."

"It does." My shoes had been soaked more than once because someone let go of the hose too soon.

Summer was still grumbling as headlights appeared at the gate. The vehicle's tires made little popping noises as it rolled up next to the office.

"That's my dad," she said. "See you tomorrow?" Glancing only at Roy and me, she added, "Nine o'clock?"

"Right," I said.

She jogged to her dad's car and, with a last wave, got inside.

The taillights hadn't even cleared the gate yet when Packrat said, "I can't get the fox call out of my head. Want to check the den in the morning?"

"Sure! And we'll check the memory card, too," I said. "Stay at my place, both of you, so I can wake you up at six-thirty."

Roy tapped the fire ring with his boot, settling the glowing red coals even more. "I'm game."

Packrat groaned. "What? Six-thirty! C'mon! You guys are killing me here."

I laughed as I took the kinked end of the water hose from Packrat's fist. Dragging it, and the rest of the hose, closer to the fire, I said, "I'll have to be back to start work at nine. It always takes half an hour to get you out of bed and awake enough to walk. We'll be lucky to be at the den for seven-thirty!"

Packrat shook his head. "Okay, fine. Wake me at six-thirty."

I held up the kinked hose. "Six. And if I can't wake you up—" I let the hose go, timing it so the spray of water just missed the end of his nose on its way to the campfire ring.

"Hey!" he laugh-yelled, jumping back from the stream of water.

"Shoulda hit him!" Roy scoffed.

The fire went dark for a second, the instant the stream of water hit. Hissing and popping, the red coals fought to stay lit. I moved the hose so the water would chase the flames, hitting them every time they tried to relight. Thick black steam rose into the air.

"I'll call Summer to meet us—"

"No!" Packrat went from laughing to serious in a heartbeat. "Just us this time."

I glanced at Roy. His eyebrows shot so high, they almost looked cartoonish.

"Okaaaaaay," I said.

Roy agreed, saying, "Just us guys this time."

I nodded. But I still had no clue why Packrat was making such a big deal about Summer.

Chapter 11

A fox den has a main entrance that is about three feet wide, with one or two escape holes, and it's lined with grasses and dry leaves.

It took an extra-large mug of hot cocoa, with the little marshmallows on top, to get Packrat out from under the covers at sunrise. Then one more before Roy and I got him into my kitchen.

Mom had just filled her mug with coffee when Roy slid a Thermos mug across the counter. Mom hesitated.

"Coffee?" Mom looked at his cup, as if he'd asked for mud. "I don't know—"

Packrat's eyes finally opened all the way. "Coffee? Yuck!"

"Coffee," Mom repeated. She shook her head, but filled Roy's outstretched travel mug with the dark, steamy liquid.

After promising Mom we'd be back at nine to start working at turning on the water, my friends and I walked down the road, out the driveway, and took a sharp left onto the red-blazed trail. More green shoots sprouted out of the ground, here and there along the footpath. Buds popped up on the maple trees, too. But for the most part, the woods still looked brown.

For a while we walked in silence, each lost in our own thoughts. Roy broke it first.

"Have you heard from Warden Kate yet?"

I nodded, and took another sip of my three-packet hot cocoa. "She e-mailed last night." Sidestepping a bunch of broken sticks on the ground, I added, "She said we were right. The trap didn't kill the fox; the coyote did. Still, she's worried, 'cause someone is poaching in the area, and they're on private property. This guy—"

"Or girl," Packrat said. We both looked at him. He shrugged, "Just sayin'."

"Or girl"—I gave him a sideways look to let him know I didn't totally agree—"isn't playing by the rules."

Roy laughed. "You sure do have it out for her."

"I do not!" Packrat shoved Roy's shoulder. "I just think we wouldn't be very good wardens if we didn't explore all the options, and possible suspects. Summer is one."

Roy put up two hands. "For the record, I think you're right—about exploring all the options. But I don't think Summer did it. I mean, what's she done to make you think that?"

"Okay, not her exactly. But, her dad. Think about it!" Packrat started walking backward, still talking in earnest. "She won't tell us exactly what he does. She won't let us come over to her house, ever. Aaaaand, she and the warden had a private conversation."

"*Shhhh!* We're getting close," I told Roy and Packrat. Partly because we were. And partly because I was done talking about Summer and her dad.

The three of us now moved very slowly, only stepping on the soft pine needles. One step on crunchy leaves would let the fox family know we were coming. Stalking foxes is way harder than stalking nesting eagles. With eagles, they sit up high and you can still see them. Foxes are low. Their red coats blend in with the dead leaves on the ground. They can go into their burrow and not come out for a long time.

When we reached the hedge of thick bushes, I looked through the trees toward the den, which was about half a football field's length away. Not seeing the kits or their mom, but remembering the fox calls from last night, I frowned. Had someone or something gotten to them?

I shook off the bad feeling. They'd probably heard us coming.

"What am I looking for?" Packrat whispered, reminding me that my friends hadn't been here with me yet.

"See that hole at the top of the hill?"

Packrat fumbled in his pockets until he found two pairs of binoculars. He gave one to Roy. "For an up-close look," he explained.

"There's an opening on the bottom right, too, but I think they mostly use the one at the top, 'cause it has a dirt shelf. Then over there," I whispered, pointing about ten feet to the left, at the top of the hill, "is another opening."

"So you've only seen them the one time?" Packrat still had the binoculars to his eyes.

"Yep. I knew something lived here, but I wasn't sure—oh! Here comes one."

Two triangle-shaped, black-tipped ears appeared, followed by two dark brown eyes in a rusty-red face. Then, a pointy black nose. Finally, the kit's whole furry face appeared.

"Awwww!" Roy breathed.

The little kit put its paws just outside the den opening. Suddenly, it scrambled out, turned, and crouched next to the hole. When the next kit came out, the first pounced! Pinning its littler sibling down, it nipped at its ears as a third kit came out to watch the wrestling match.

The fourth kit poked its head out, too. The first two rolled down the hill, head over tail. They broke apart, shook off, then trotted up to the dirt ledge like the best of friends.

"I thought you said there were five?" Packrat asked.

"Probably too scared," I assured him. But after fifteen minutes, when the fifth one hadn't come out to wrestle with the others, I frowned. Had we lost one already?

Suddenly, all four kits went still. Their heads, one by one, turned to the right.

"The mom?" Packrat scanned the woods with his binoculars.

The sound of crunching leaves cutting through the woods told me it couldn't be the mother fox. She never made that much noise. No, these

were human footsteps. I looked at my watch. At seven in the morning? Who would be out here?

The footsteps came closer. One short, sharp bark came from our left.

"That's the mom!" I whispered, as two kits followed her orders, ducking back into the den.

The footsteps stopped, but another bark rang out. One more kit silently slunk to the safety of its home.

After a minute of no sound, the kit who hadn't listened to his mother took a step away from the den. A burst of orange bounded through the woods from the left. The kit's head whipped around to look, then it scampered into the den. The white tip of its tail was the last thing we saw.

The whole time, not even a leaf crackled. Boy, were those foxes quiet!

The footsteps started up again. As they neared, I saw a flash of green, which would have blended in if it hadn't been April in Maine. Something white. No, yellow. Blue. Jeans.

"It's Summer!" Packrat whispered.

"Summer?" I said. "She must be worried about the kits, too."

"Does she go out on your property without you a lot?" Packrat asked, all innocent-like. But there was a challenge underneath.

I didn't want an argument, so I let the question hang there. Summer hummed low as she walked, but loud enough that we could hear her. She stopped to look toward the opening and, not seeing anything, her face fell. When she kept walking toward it, I put my hands on the ground to stand, but Packrat pulled me down.

"Let's see what she's up to," he said.

I sat back down. "Fine!"

She moved to the trail cam and opened it up. I couldn't see exactly what she was doing, because the open door was in the way of the control panel. Was she pushing buttons? Taking out the memory card? Erasing everything?

No, Summer wouldn't do that. Packrat was just making me think the worst.

I jumped up. "Summer!" I whisper-yelled. "Over here!"

She jumped, stumbled, and turned. Seeing me, she put a hand over her heart, shutting the cam quickly.

I used both hands to motion her over to the bushes. "*Shhhh!*"

From the corner of my eye, I saw Roy and Packrat give each other a look.

"I didn't know you guys were here!" Summer whispered, making her way over to us and getting behind the hedge.

She frowned back at the cam. "I got here early and your store was closed, so I thought, What the heck? Maybe there's something on the memory card that'll show why the fox yelled last night."

I shot Packrat a told-you-so look.

He shot me a it-doesn't-prove-a-thing look.

I held out my hand, but Summer shook her head. "You scared me! And called me over. I didn't get it. Want me to go back?"

"Nah." I didn't meet Packrat's eyes, because I chose to believe Summer. "We'll get it later."

"Anything happening?" she asked.

"We saw four kits, 'til you came barreling through the woods," Packrat said.

"I didn't barrel!"

"*Shhhh!*" we all said.

We sat, watched, and waited. Finally, we were rewarded with two black ears. I looked quickly at Summer. She made a motion to zip her lips, which almost had Roy laughing out loud.

Then came the nose and the round face, until it stood all the way out again. This time, though, it sat. And it looked. Not at us, but into the woods. The tip of its pink tongue flicked out to touch its own nose. A second kit came out to sit nearby. Together the two whined like puppies.

"Awwww," Summer whispered.

The kits nosed around under the leaves nearest them. A third one came out of the den.

"Why are they crying?" Packrat asked me. "Hungry?"

"I don't know. Foxes keep their food stockpiled in caches, so I don't think so. They probably just miss their mom." I checked my watch. Quarter of eight. "And we're probably keeping her from coming back. We need a blind." Looking around, I saw a level spot, with a clear view to the den. "Something we can set up and leave up. Something we can get inside and see the kits without them seeing us."

"Great idea!" Summer's voice sent the kits scampering back into the den.

"Can you soundproof it, too?" Packrat asked.

Roy and I laughed.

Summer did not.

As Roy and Packrat brainstormed about what we'd need, Summer moved closer to me.

"There's only four," she said. "Are you worried?"

Was I worried? Yeah. Nature could be harsh. There were lots of predators who'd grab a kit, given the chance.

A little brown head popped up in the opening. Chocolate-brown eyes locked on mine.

But it was a two-legged predator that was giving me the funny feeling in the pit of my stomach.

Chapter 12

Foxes can hear underground prey, digging, eating, rustling. They'll eagerly dig it up, hoping to find a meal.

Vern, Summer, and I met at the campground workshop to load up the tools we'd need for our first job of the day. Packrat had gone back to his camper with Roy, for breakfast. They said they'd meet us at nine o'clock at the campsite with the fallen tree.

Vern gave one sharp whistle.

"Calling Bo?" Summer asked, shading her eyes and looking up to the sky.

"He's never far away." Vern stepped up beside me as I flipped through my keys to find the silver, square one that unlocked the workshop door.

"He doesn't just fly off?" I asked.

"Too used to people."

I heard the flapping of wings before I saw Bo. The raven landed on my shoulder, then tipped his head down and to one side, eyeing the keys in my hand.

"These are mine. Get your own," I teased.

Cruuuuuck!

"Summer, can you grab some rakes and shovels?" I pointed to the outside wall, where they all hung upside down against the building. "And put them in the back of the golf cart?"

"Sure!"

I slid my key in the workshop lock, twisted, and swung the door wide, all with Bo still on my shoulder. The second the lights came on, Bo hop-flew off my shoulder, across the room, to the wooden bench.

"Uh-oh." Vern made a grab for his pet. Bo hopped away, pecking first at a nail, then at a round, metal, water clamp. "This place is a gold mine to a raven." He whistled. Bo looked reluctant, but one more insistent whistle from Vern had Bo flying back to his shoulder. "I'd better get him out of here."

I grabbed the truck keys Vern would need and handed them to him. I added Dad's big gas-powered chain saw to the back of the golf cart, along with the little electric one. Then I went back and grabbed the golf cart keys for me before shutting the door behind us.

"I think that's it," I said.

Vern climbed in the dump truck driver's seat, slamming the door shut behind him. Seeing Bo perched on the back of the passenger seat, I smiled. But when Vern adjusted the side mirror and started the truck, I felt a heaviness on my shoulders. No one else had ever driven our dump truck. Except maybe Mom, and she didn't really like to because she said it didn't have good visibility, and she was afraid she'd back up over something. Or someone. My dad would roll his eyes and ask, "So what will you do if your mom-van breaks down and you have to go into town? Or what if I get sick and you have to help some camper?" To which Mom always laughed lightly, before giving him a kiss on the cheek as if to say, *Like that would ever happen!*

Yeah.

Sitting on the golf cart seat, with Summer next to me on the passenger side, I sighed heavily before flipping the black lever to reverse. Backing out of the parking spot, I pulled up alongside Vern.

"Follow me," I called. Moving the lever to forward, I led the way to Raccoon Trail.

I thought I had a clear memory of the scene of Dad's accident, but the tree that'd knocked him down and taken his memory from us for a couple of hours was waaaay bigger than I remembered. Packrat and Roy were already standing in front of it, branches towering over them. What a mess, too! Branches large and small had broken or burst in the fall. Pine boughs scattered like an extreme game of 52 Pickup.

I blinked fast, so my friends wouldn't see my eyes watering. How had Dad survived?

Packrat's wave and Roy's giant grin brought my smile back. Boy, did I have cool friends. Who else would be all excited about a week's worth of chores? Not just chores—jobs. Hard jobs.

Summer was cool, too, but she had no idea what she was getting into. Roy and Packrat knew every inch of the campground. They knew how hard my dad worked around here. They knew it wouldn't be easy to get the place ready to open. But, heck, they were here.

I drove the golf cart onto the site, as close as I could get to the fallen tree, looking everywhere but at the spot my dad had fallen. The sooner we cleaned this mess up, the sooner I could try to forget how my goof had almost cost Dad his life.

Roy and Packrat went to either side of the tailgate on the dump truck, unhitched its hooks, and let it drop with a bang that echoed up and down the empty street. Summer brought them each a rake.

"We don't start with that," Packrat said, waving it off. "We have to cut the trunk and limbs first. Raking comes last."

Summer looked at the rake. "Well, how was I supposed to know?" She tossed her ponytail from side to side as she huffed her way back to the golf cart and stood the rakes up against it.

"Give her a break," I said. "With the extra person, we'll get done quicker, which means we'll be able to go and grab the memory card sooner."

Vern walked around to the golf cart. "Memory card?" he asked.

I handed him some gloves from the front seat. "Yeah. I have a trail camera pointed on the fox den. We're hoping it'll show us what the fox was all upset about last night."

Vern put one glove on, then the other.

"Hmm," he said, wiggling his fingers, getting the gloves just so. "Sometimes they aren't in distress when they make that call, you know. I once saw a fox, well, a *video* of a fox, and it sat on a rock, hollering like that. But it seemed more like it was trying to make contact with another fox."

I tipped my head to the side. "I hope that's all it was."

"Just make sure you don't go to the den too much. The mom might just up and move those kits. I'd wait a couple weeks to go again, if I was you—maybe a month." He smiled at me. "But they're tons of fun to watch, aren't they?"

"Hey!" Summer turned to us all, eyes dancing with excitement. "Guess what I saw online last night? A news report that a trail camera in Yosemite National Park picked up some pictures of a Sierra Nevada red fox! There's, like, less than sixty of them in the United States, and it's the first time one's been seen in a hundred years, and they're one of the rarest mammals—"

Thwack! Thwack!

We all turned toward the noise. Packrat held two heavy gloves, banging them together.

"What?" he asked, when he looked up to see us all staring at him. "I was banging the dirt out of them." He slid one glove on, then the other, much like Vern had.

Considering they looked brand-new, I wasn't buying it.

"Well, I think it's cool, what Summer said. Wish our foxes were Sierras."

"Oh," Packrat said. He kept fiddling with his gloves. "I guess I wasn't listening. I was thinking about how foxes can hear the annoying squeak of a mouse from over three hundred feet away."

Roy and I looked back to Summer, who'd put her hands on her hips, staring at Packrat like she was an eagle, talons held straight out for his head. "And did you know," she said, the words coming slowly and carefully, "that foxes mark their territories with urine?"

Roy laughed out loud, doubling over. "She . . . she . . . urine!"

Packrat frowned. He opened his mouth, but Vern spoke first.

"I'll cut," he said, lifting the big gas chain saw out of the back of the golf cart. "You four toss the logs and branches in the back of the truck, okay?"

I gave him a grateful look. I hated seeing my friends go back and forth like that.

I lifted the little electric chain saw out of the golf cart, trying to make it look like I'd handled it a hundred times before, when I'd only done it four. Okay, two. With Dad right next to me.

"I'll cut all the little branches. That'll give you room to get to the trunk."

Vern paused, with his hand on the puller of the gas chain saw. He looked at mine, then at the tree, then back at me. He hesitated. Packrat pulled eye-protecting goggles from his coat and handed a pair to me and a second pair to Vern. "Safety first, right?"

"Riiiiight," Vern said slowly, kinda like he didn't really want to wear them at all. Neither did I, but if it gave me a chance to help cut branches, to do some real work—work that'd make my dad proud of me again—then I'd wrap myself up in bubble wrap five times over.

Vern pulled the cord on his saw once, twice, three times, before it roared to life. Bo flew to a nearby branch, strutting back and forth, watching. When Vern had adjusted the saw so it didn't race, he turned to the downed tree. Roy gave me a thumbs-up. Packrat clapped me on the back. As my own little electric saw roared, Packrat yelled in my ear, "Be careful! Your mom will kill us if you get hurt!"

Words my dad had said more than once. He wasn't here, but yet, he was.

With all the noise from the saws and stuff, no one spoke. The sun rose higher and higher, until it was almost straight above us. The temperature of the day got hotter and hotter. I'd thrown off my sweatshirt an hour ago, and now I ran my shirtsleeve over my forehead, wiping the sweat away before it dripped in my eyes. Sure didn't feel like April; more like late June. Not that I was complaining or anything.

I grabbed a cold bottle of water from the cooler Mom had sent with us and twisted the cap off. Summer joined me, reaching in to lift a dripping wet bottle out. I'd just put my bottle to my lips and begun to guzzle when Packrat called, "Hey! Toss me one?"

"Sure!" Summer said, before I could. She set down her bottle and grabbed another, twisting the cap, but not taking it off.

I lowered my bottle slowly, trying to catch her eye. What was she up to?

Packrat tossed the log he'd carried over into the back of the truck, then swiped his shirtsleeve over his forehead.

"Ready?" Summer called sweetly.

"Hey," I said quickly, "I don't think—"

She tossed the bottle. Midair, the cap came off, and the bottle went end over end, spraying water in every direction. When Packrat caught it, he looked up at her, water dripping from his hair, his nose, and his chin.

I couldn't help it. I grinned from ear to ear. Seeing Packrat eyeing me, I threw my hands up.

"Not me," I protested.

"Gotcha." Summer tipped up her chin, eyes sparkling. "That's for soaking my sneakers with the hose last night!"

"You know," Packrat said, no hint of a smile on his face, "this means war."

Just as serious, Summer answered, "I'm counting on it."

Just then, my radio crackled and little-girl giggles came through. Bo flew down to land on my shoulder as I pushed the button to answer.

"Molly?"

Bo tipped his head toward me, almost like he was listening in.

"What's up?" I asked.

More giggles before her voice came through loud and clear. "Mom says come and eat."

I tried to answer, but Molly still had her finger on her button. I heard Mom talking. Then a voice that sounded like Cat Lady's. I frowned down at the radio.

Packrat came up beside me. I held out the radio for him and Roy and Summer to listen, too.

Lots of words I couldn't quite hear, but voices were getting louder. Even mad.

Then we heard, "Something has to be done!" More mumbling, then, ". . . screaming all night."

A soothing voice butted in, Mom maybe.

It *was* Cat Lady, talking right over her.

"Fred . . ."—mumble, mumble—". . . missing since last night!"

"Probably just hunting—"

"—never not come home before. I've searched everywhere! That fox is responsible, and I'm warning you right now—"

My friends and I exchanged worried glances.

"—I won't let it get the rest of my cats!"

Chapter 13

*Red foxes stand about fifteen inches tall, are
approximately forty inches long from nose to tip
of tail, and weigh anywhere between seven
and twenty pounds.*

I didn't know about Packrat and Roy, but it was kinda hard for me
to get out of bed the next morning because I was groggy-tired, and my
shoulders and upper arms hurt, too. Not only had we cut and stacked
that fallen tree for most of the day the day before, but when we'd finished that job, I'd had a bright idea. We dug out an old, faded, green
canvas tent which had been hanging around the workshop since before
my parents bought the place. Laying it out on my front lawn, we'd
randomly spray-painted gray and brown spots, giving it a camouflaged
look. Then we'd hiked into the woods with the poles and stakes to set
it up on a flat space, where we had a good view of the fox den—close,
but not too close. By the time we were done, it was dusk, so we didn't
even have time to test out our new fox blind. I would have been wicked
disappointed, except Summer and Packrat hadn't said a word to each
other the whole time.

Their silence had been louder than the sound of the tree dropping.

Now, Mom was standing in front of the whiteboard on the office
wall. She reached up with a marker to draw a red line through the black
words CUT UP FALLEN TREE / PICK UP BRANCHES IN ROADS. I'm glad she
didn't erase them, because I just wanted to stare at them. A reminder
that we'd tackled the job, and won.

"Top of my to-do list today is to put in some orders so the deliver-
ies can arrive before opening day. Ice cream—"

"Cookie sandwiches!" Packrat licked his lips.

"Strawberry crunch!" Molly called.

"Fudge bars," I said quickly, as Mom grabbed paper and pen. I didn't want her to forget my favorite. Or Dad's. "And the caramel sundae cups." Mom shot me a smile. She knew his favorite, too.

"Pints of chocolate," Roy said firmly.

Mom's hand hovered over the paper, as she looked at him. "Pints? You eat a whole pint?"

"With the little wooden spoons," he said, with a nod.

Mom wrote it down, asking Vern, "Do you have a favorite?"

"I like plain old chocolate-covered vanilla on a stick."

Mom smiled down at her paper. "That's my favorite, too. I'll call this in later, along with ice, bread, chips, soda—"

Roy opened his mouth, but Mom put up a hand. "Trust me, I know what all your favorites are in the drink department. I got this. You all need to get started on getting water to bathrooms and campsites."

"Get water to them?" Vern paused, the Thermos mug of coffee he'd brought with him halfway to his mouth. "Doesn't it come from the same place you get your store and house water?"

"We have two wells," Mom explained.

I butted in, saying, "The one that was here when we got here feeds the house and the store and the sites on the main road. Those all have piping for winter water; they won't freeze up."

Mom finished, "The second one, we use for summer campsites, bathrooms, pool, and everything else." Mom smiled. "My husband always worries about having enough water. Even with two very good wells, he still insisted on fixing up the old water tower—"

"That's yours?" Vern looked impressed. "I can just make out the top of it through the woods, from my site. I didn't realize your property went way back there."

Mom nodded. "It's the highest point we have. We fill that tank from the well, so we have water in reserve in case of a power outage. The campground can't be open without water. So," Mom grabbed her clipboard off the counter, handing it to Vern, "Jim listed the steps we have to take." Moving to the whiteboard, she wrote the rest of the jobs in black marker.

"Pour bleach in the wells," Vern read out loud from Dad's list as she wrote. "Let sit twenty-four to seventy-two hours to kill the germs in the water lines. Then open all the spigots—"

"One hundred and thirty-two of them!" Roy said.

Vern kept reading, "Check water lines between sites?"

"For splits and leaking from frost or freezing," Packrat explained.

"We just walk it," I added. "No big deal."

"But . . . well, this is more than a day's worth of work." Vern's eyebrows met in the middle, as he studied the list.

"Is that a problem?" Mom frowned at his frown.

I felt a stone of worry in my stomach. *We had a deal; you can't back out now!*

"No, not a problem exactly," Vern said. "I guess I hadn't thought there'd be this much work to turn on the water. It's time-consuming, isn't it?" He seemed lost in thought. "I wonder . . . if I move that—" He looked up, a startled look in his eyes. "Oh! I was just . . . thinking out loud. I didn't mean to worry you. The appointments, with the specialists—for my leg, you know. I can reschedule them. I'll make it work. I gave you my word."

Mom looked relieved. "So you need to take an afternoon or two off—that's not a problem. Keep your appointments." When Vern started to protest, she held up a hand. "No, I insist. Each one of your references said you were a great worker, very honest. I trust you."

"Okay, then," Vern tipped back his mug, drained it, and set it on the counter. "I'll give you a list of those dates. I'm here now, though, so let's get to it. Sounds like we need the golf cart, a toolbox—"

Toolbox! I groaned. "I never went back for the toolbox! It's got all the water-connection stuff in it," I said. "We're gonna need it."

"Where's that?" Packrat asked.

"In the shed, by the water tower." *Where Dad left it,* I added to myself.

Vern opened his Thermos mug and poured more coffee into it. "How about I go and collect it, while you pour the bleach—"

Thinking of his leg, and the climb up the hill to the tower, I quickly said, "We'll go. You do the bleach."

"The valve is there, in the shed, to open the water line to the tank," Mom said to me. "Remember where?" When I nodded, she said, "Good. That way it'll fill when you turn the water on down here."

I signaled to Packrat and Roy. It was time to go. We headed out of the office.

Suddenly, a hand took mine. A little one.

"Cooper? Can I go?"

Molly. I looked down. "Not right now, Squirt."

Her face drooped, and her eyes shone with unshed tears. Darn it.

I looked at Packrat and Roy, who'd come out behind me. They both shrugged. I sighed.

"Okay, Squirt. Let's go."

We hadn't gone more than a few steps when Mom called, "And Cooper?"

I turned.

"Come right back. Don't leave Vern waiting."

A sudden flashback hit me—Dad standing by the truck at the workshop, digging around behind the seat:

> *Darn it. Cooper, I left my gloves in the shed.*
> *Which shed?*
> *The one at the tower. I left the water-connection*
> *toolbox, and they're in it. Could you go grab them?*

*Actually, grab the whole box. We're going to need it when
I turn on the water in a couple of days. I'll meet you by the
tree I marked for cutting yesterday. The one on Raccoon Trail.*

Got it, Dad! I'd said, happy to take a short hike with
Summer, who'd paddled over to visit and help for the day.

And Cooper? Dad had asked.

Yeah?

*Come right back. Don't leave me waiting, okay? I need
to cut and clear the tree today.*

Promise, Dad! I'd called, thinking he'd never know if we
made a quick stop at the fox den to get the memory card.
It'd only add five or ten minutes, tops.

Now, I hung my head as I walked away so the guys wouldn't see
the tears prickling.

Chapter 14

Fox tracks can be found along the edges of fields and forests. Foxes walk in a straight line, and their prints are one and a half to two inches long, with hair marks between the toes.

I watched Molly as we walked single file on the red-blazed trail. Something was bugging her—and it wasn't mayflies. Usually when we hiked, whether it was with Mom and Dad up Bradbury Mountain, or just the two of us by the lake, she would race ahead. She'd sing at the top of her lungs. She'd talk your ear off about nothing at all. She would clear the trail of wildlife, long before I could see any of it.

But today, she didn't do any of those things. For one thing, she was staying by my side. What's more, she wasn't talking at all.

Weird.

When we got to the giant boulder, where we usually took a right to go off-trail to the fox den, Packrat looked back at me. I pointed to the left.

"But—" he looked longingly to the right "I thought that's why you volunteered to go to the tower."

I shook my head, trying to hold firm. "We have to get back to Vern."

Roy muttered under his breath, something like "Vern can wait."

"But turning on the water can't." I tried to sound like Dad, when he meant business.

Packrat nudged Roy forward on the trail. Molly took my hand.

After we'd hiked another ten minutes, the path forked. We took this right and the trail immediately went upward, to the top of a mid-size hill. Molly called it a mountain, but it wasn't. Not quite.

Cooper and Packrat: Mystery of the Missing Fox

As we took the last couple of steps and reached the top, a flat, open area came into view. It was the highest point on our property. Across the clearing and to the far right, against the tree line, stood a forest-green water tower, the tank round in shape, with a slightly slanted, metal roof. Dad had painted it to blend in with the rest of the forest. I joked with him that it looked like a giant acorn on four legs.

In the middle of the roof stood a four-foot-tall lightning rod. From that, a wire ran to the left side of the clearing, over a duck pond, and down to a small, square brick shed. The wire really didn't do anything anymore; once it had carried electricity to the tower for a water-level gauge. Dad just didn't want to take it down, in case he decided to use the gauge again.

I took the key ring off my belt and pawed through the keys, one by one, until I found a little round-headed gold one. Sliding it into the lock hanging off the latch on the door, I turned it. *Click.*

I looked back at my friends. They stood at the edge of the duck pond with Molly, squatting down, peering past rocks and grass, pointing into the water. I knew they were looking for frogs. And not just any frog. My three-legged frog, Oscar.

I wanted to join them in the worst way, but I couldn't get distracted again. Not until I got what I'd come for. I stepped into the shed, blinking several times until my eyes adjusted to the dim light coming through the little windows. Mainly, the shed held a few tools for when Dad worked on the tower, and a portable ladder to lean against it, so he could climb up to the catwalk that went around the whole thing. I'd asked Dad once why he didn't just put a permanent ladder on the side of the tower. That way he could climb up without lugging the ladder back and forth or worrying about locking it up.

"It'd be easier," I'd said.

His reply was, "Exactly." It'd taken me three days to figure out he'd meant that he didn't want it to be easier. Especially for my friends and me to climb.

Like that stopped us.

In the back corner was the valve to the tower. With it, we filled the tank in the spring, and drained it every fall, so it wouldn't freeze and split in the bitter cold.

Remembering Dad's directions, I pressed down on the valve, and waited to hear the *whoosh* of air once it opened. Then I turned the dial to the ON position. Now, when we turned on the water from the well, the water would stream through to fill the tank at the top of the tower.

I turned. Sitting on the dirt floor, lit up by a faint sunbeam shining through a little window, was Dad's open toolbox.

"There you are," I whispered.

I picked up his large leather gloves, black in the palm and fingertips from months of use. I put them on. They were big. But they made me feel a little bit like Dad was with me. I closed the box, grabbed it by its handle, and stepped through the doorway.

"Cooper!" Roy waved me over. "Check this out."

Walking over, I set the toolbox in the grass and crouched down to look. Fox prints. They led around the duck pond, turning to come back and retrace themselves.

Ribbit! Ribbit!

A small green frog sat sunning himself at the edge of the pond.

Ribbit!

Foxes ate frogs.

"Any sign of Oscar?" I asked hopefully.

Packrat shook his head. "Not yet. But it's early. We'll come back."

I nodded. Putting a hand to my eyes, I scanned the pond. Every October, I brought Oscar here, so he could burrow in the mud and spend the winter the way he was supposed to. My mother's garden pond, where he lived in the summer, wasn't deep enough. I knew I was taking a big chance. Especially since he only had three legs and couldn't hop really well.

I sighed.

Roy took off running. "Last one to the top has to cluck like a chicken from the top of the playground climber."

"Wait! Wait, wait, wait!" I ordered. Packrat froze, halfway to the tower. Roy was already at one of the tower legs, hands above his head, grabbing hold, stepping up using the crossbars that formed Xs in it.

Roy's face got all confused, then his eyes flashed in annoyance. He took a step down to point at me.

"Are you going all adult on us?" he taunted. "First, you won't go to the den, and now you won't let us climb? Just 'cause we're doing your dad's chores doesn't mean we can't have a little fun, you know."

Packrat looked between the two of us. "Roy," he warned. "That wasn't . . . wasn't . . ."

I stormed toward the two of them. Just when I got within a few feet of Roy, I yelled, "Gotcha!" and sprinted to a third leg of the tower.

"Cooper! No!" Molly cried.

"Done it a hundred times, Molly!"

I grabbed hold of the tower leg, put one foot on the first X, and started climbing.

"You're too high!" Molly called up, eyes wide.

I didn't stop, but smiled down at her to show we were having fun.

When I reached the top of the metal leg, on which the water tank sat, I reached out and around to grab hold of the catwalk, pulling myself onto it. Once there, I stood up and had to shuffle-slide my feet with my back against the tank, until I reached the small ladder going up to the top edge of the tower. It was the only way up to the roof of the tank, where we'd find the hatch to look inside. So, as I climbed hand over hand, I knew I wouldn't be clucking like a chicken on the playground climber.

Roy groaned in frustration behind me, but not as loud as Packrat did behind him.

Up I went, hands on the sides of the ladder, feet on the rungs, until I touched the roof with my hands. The shingles were made from really long sheets of metal, lying one on top of the other. They'd been there so long, the edges were a little rough and bent up in some places. I'd torn more than one pair of jeans crawling over them.

Crawling to the middle of the roof, I stood, raised my hands in the air, and slowly turned in a circle. Being up here always made me feel like I was king of the world. Or of Wilder Family Campground, anyway. Roy joined me and we both laughed when Packrat's head came up over the edge, his eyes rolling at our victory dance. Once he joined us, we stood side by side, gazing out over the treetops to see Pine Lake.

Molly shaded her eyes, looking up at us from the ground.

"What do you see?" she called. Curiosity had won out over fear.

"Pine Lake," I called back. "And Ant Island."

"The loons?"

"No, they're too far—"

I broke off as Packrat started digging in first one pocket, then another. I grinned.

"You know, you're a faster climber than me. The weight of that coat keeps ya from beating me."

He shrugged. "I could peel it off before I climb, but then you wouldn't have these," he said, pulling binoculars from his pocket.

I scanned the lake. "Two teeny, tiny loons swimming and diving together," I called down to Molly.

Roy pointed to the bright blue sky. "Eagle?"

"Yep!" I said. "Landing in the nest. Hey! Looks like it's feeding chicks! They must have just hatched! Cool!"

"Okay, Cooper! Come down now!" Molly called up. She bit her thumbnail.

"Hold on! I've gotta check the inside."

Almost directly in the middle of the roof, there was a small wooden hatch with a latch. Kneeling down next to it, I pushed the round metal latch to the side and flipped it down. Then I opened the door. Packrat offered me his flashlight.

"How's it look?" he asked.

"No holes? Anything dead?" Roy joked.

I rolled my eyes. That's exactly what I was looking for. I ran the flashlight up and down all the walls.

"Looks good," I said. I closed it up before walking over to the ladder with Roy. My mind was already on getting back to Vern, completing all the steps to get the water on and this tank filled.

"Umm, Cooper?" Packrat pointed down into the woods. I raised my binoculars. There was movement, something blue and red. It was hard to see as the figure made its way through the trees. On the trail? Finally, it stepped right where we could see it through an opening.

"Cat Lady," I said, lowering the binoculars and going into a crouch.

"She's carrying something," Packrat added.

Molly looked to the woods behind her. "I hear something."

I put a finger to my lips. Cat Lady finding us here was something I didn't want to happen. She'd ask a thousand questions and try to get the location of the fox den out of us again. Or she might follow us back to it!

"Molly," I whispered as loud as I dared. "Hide in the shed!"

"Why?" she whisper-yelled back.

"Umm . . . 'cause—" I looked at Packrat.

"We're playing hide-and-seek," he said.

Molly gave us a yeah-right look, but she headed toward the shed anyway.

"Hit the deck," Roy warned.

My friends and I lay on the roof of the water tower, warm from the sun. When I knew Molly had shut the door to the shed, I crawled over to where I could watch the section of trail that passed by the bottom of the hill. You couldn't see from here, but it cut through part of the soggy, blueberry-bush section of land, before winding around to the other side of the lake. Cat Lady wasn't going to get very far. If she didn't know it already, she'd have to turn back when she reached that part of the trail.

She was almost at the base of the hill now. Every few steps, she'd stop and call, "Fred? Fred?" Then she'd click her tongue. When her shoulders drooped, I felt kind of bad for her. She must miss Fred an awful lot if she was way out here looking for him. She continued walking, only to stop a few more feet away and do it all over again.

"What's that she's got?" Packrat whispered, seeing a crate-like box hanging from her hand.

"A cat carrier, I think."

She passed by our mountain. Roy and Packrat started to get up, but I raised my hand in a stay-there-for-a-minute kind of way. It wasn't long before she came back by, muttering to herself. She called for Fred again. Silence.

"Fox?" she cried. "You've got my Fred! I know it! I'm coming for you!"

Chapter 15

*Coyotes, wolves, and humans pose the greatest threat
to a red fox, but young kits can also fall prey to dogs,
eagles, and badgers.*

"We have to get back to the office," I protested. Didn't my friends
get it? Of course I wanted to check on the fox kits! Especially after hearing Cat Lady's threat. But we'd already eaten up a lot of time hiding out
on the water tower, waiting for her to leave the area.

"Did she mean it?" Molly had asked, after we'd climbed down
from the tower to join her on the ground.

"Nah," I'd said, pretending to brush off the whole weird incident
like a moose brushes off a fly.

But, yeah. Yeah, I think she did.

"C'mon!" Roy argued. "We won't let you stop and watch. Just a
quick walk-by to check the blind."

"I know you wanna get back," Packrat reasoned with me. "But
Roy's right—it's only three, four minutes out of our way."

Molly took my hand and looked up at me with her best, please-
please-please-do-it-for-me look.

"Okay!" I ran my fingers through my hair. But this was what had
gotten me into trouble in the first place. Not being able to resist seeing
what lived there. "But you can't let me stop. For more than five minutes,
anyway. Promise."

"Promise," Molly said, and she let go of my hand to skip on ahead.

The sun had disappeared, and dark clouds peeked over the hori-
zon. Rain? That wouldn't help get the chores done. Then again, Dad
always worked in the rain. It never stopped him.

Only one thing had stopped him.

We walked along the trail until we got to the fork with the big boulder.

"Molly!" I whispered loudly.

She turned. Somewhere along the way, she'd picked up a branch to use as a walking stick. I pointed to let her know we were going the other way. She smiled and skipped back to join us.

"Why are you so happy?" I whispered, putting a hand on her head and gently turning her down the right path.

In a happy whisper, she shot over her shoulder, " 'Cause you're taking me with you to see the foxes!"

Could it be that simple? Seeing Molly shoot me another happy smile over her shoulder, I decided it could.

When we got close, Roy and Packrat and I helped Molly watch for crunchy spots and branches. Now I really, really wanted to see those kits and the mom fox, for Molly's sake.

When we reached the blind, I let Molly go in the tent first, so she could look out the screened-in window. I climbed in second, then Packrat and Roy. We were squished, but we fit.

Molly gasped and pulled my sweatshirt sleeve. "I think I see one!"

I looked, but I didn't see what she was looking at.

"That white thing?" Molly insisted.

I crouched down behind her. This time, my eyes followed her pointing finger to a heap of white on top of the bank, over the den opening.

"The kits are brownish reddish now," I whispered, as Molly leaned into me to hear. "That's not them."

"Oh." She sighed.

"It looks like a towel," Roy said.

"Clothes?" Packrat offered.

I crawled toward the opening. "I'll check it out."

Even standing outside the blind, I still couldn't tell what the white bundle was. Should I get it out of there? Or was it too soon after our last visit? If I did go, I could grab the memory card from the cam—

Wait a minute.

"Where's the trail camera?" I whispered.

Packrat shaded his eyes, scanning the area. Roy frowned. "Are we in the right spot?" he asked.

But that was one of those I-know-I'm-right questions. We were in the watching spot. We were looking at the fox den. And the camera was in front of the fox den. At least, it was the last time we were here.

"Maybe it fell," Packrat whispered back.

I nodded. "Yeah. Wait here, Squirt."

Vern's words rang in my head. *I'd wait a couple weeks to go again, if I was you—maybe a month.*

But I had to find out what that white thing was. What if the kits chewed on it? What if it was a clue as to who'd been poaching?

I inched my way, one small, carefully placed step at a time. I wasn't afraid for me, but I *was* scared I'd spook the kits and mom so much, she'd move them. I ran over the plan in my mind. First, I'd get the camera and the memory card. Then I'd climb the bank, walk across the top of it, and grab that . . . thing.

Reaching the tree, I practically hugged it as I stepped around it, looking down. No camera. I crouched to search under the low bushes. Nothing.

"What the heck?" I muttered, standing back up, looking further away, knowing a heavy camera wouldn't fall far. I looked back toward the blind, throwing my hands in the air silently, so as not to scare the kits. But in my mind, I screamed, *It's gone! Somebody must have stolen it!*

I kicked the tree in frustration. "Now we'll never know how that stuff got up there," I muttered.

Four little kit faces appeared in the opening. Seeing me, they retreated back into the den.

They knew I was here. I had to move quickly now.

I decided to walk left for a ways. Then I climbed the bank and walked back toward the den and the bundle. When I was only a few feet from it, I heard a sharp, short bark off through the trees to my left. Then another, closer than the first. The mother fox!

Reaching the bundle, I grabbed it and kept going, walking as quietly as I could. When I was about fifty yards from the den, I turned to walk down the hill back toward the blind. Maybe it was because I turned into the wind or I started paying attention, but all of a sudden, a horrible, sharp smell reached my nose and made it twitch. My eyes watered. I looked around, but I didn't see anything.

Except the bundle in my hand.

I dropped it on the ground like a hot potato and pinched my nose shut. I kicked the bundle once, twice. It rolled and opened like a flower. But not a pretty-smelling one, in spite of the big, bright yellow daisy on the T-shirt, which lay next to two grayish sneakers.

"Ewwww!" Packrat came out of the blind. He whipped a package of tissues out of his pocket. Pulling two or three from it, he held them over his nose. Roy pulled his sweatshirt up over his, while Molly pinched hers shut like me.

"Gross!" Roy cried.

"What the heck!" Packrat tapped one of the sneakers with his own to roll it over. "Size eight. Girls' or guys'—can you tell?"

"Why were they at the den?" Molly's voice was all funny-sounding from pinching her nose.

"No idea," I answered. The radio crackled. I groaned and gave my friends a sharp look. I knew we couldn't just take a quick look! Now I'd spent way more time here than I'd wanted to.

"Cooper?" Vern's voice. "You there?"

"Yes! Sorry! I'm on my way back now."

"No worries. It took longer than I thought to get set up, and get the chlorine in the well. But I'm good now. Did you find the toolbox?"

"Yep. In the shed, like Dad said."

I heard a girl's voice, then Vern said, "Summer says to tell you she's here." A pause, then, "Excuse me, she *just* got here."

I nodded, then remembered he couldn't see me through the radio. "Be right there."

I stared at the T-shirt. "We should take it," I said, not quite sure I really wanted to.

"I'm not carrying it!" Roy said.

We stood in a semicircle, staring down at it. The main color of the shirt was white, but there were yellow stains on it, too.

Packrat took a clothespin from his pocket and put it on his nose. Then he pulled out an extra-large ziplock bag and a disposable latex glove. Using the glove, he picked up the T-shirt and the two gray sneakers and put them in the bag, zipping it up tight.

We all released our noses to breathe in some fresh, spring air.

"You're saving them?" Molly asked.

"They're clues," I answered, leading us quickly down the trail. "Someone else has found our fox den."

Summer joined us when we dropped Molly off with Mom. Then the four of us went looking for Vern to help him dig up the underground valves, and to turn on the water to flood the water lines. *Let sit twenty-four to seventy-two hours,* Dad had written.

"Can you do the rest of the list now?" Vern asked, whistling for Bo while looking at his watch. "I have just enough time to make my one o'clock appointment."

Dad's notes explained how we should check every water spigot, on every site, for a leak. Water was a huge deal to my dad. A split in a line—heck, even a fast leak—could drain the well. It's one of the things he always says keeps him up at night. Without water, you can't keep the campground open for very long.

"This will be easy," I assured Vern. "Dad said all we have to do is walk the lines, looking for leaks. It'll take a couple hours, tops."

"Hey!" Packrat said. "Maybe we'll get out on the lake. No, back to the den! To make sure the mother didn't move the kits yet."

Bo flew in to settle on Vern's arm, a large carabiner in his beak. He looked at all of us, flew to Packrat's shoulder, and pushed it into his cheek.

"I think he's trying to give it to you," Vern said.

The raven pushed it into Packrat's cheek again.

Packrat put his pointer finger in a top pocket of his coat, right under the bird.

"Here, Bo," he said, "this is your pocket." Packrat opened it wide. "The other carabiner is there, too."

Bo dropped his treasure in, then flew back to Vern.

"Do you think he got this one from the shop, too?" I asked, trying to remember if I'd shut the door.

Vern's eyes twinkled. He lifted his pointer finger to pet Bo's chest.

"I wouldn't be surprised. He's seen the inside and knows it's full of treasure. And once you find treasure, well, it's kind of hard to resist."

As my friends and I walked the campground, from site to site, we felt pretty sure that we'd get back over to the fox den, since we'd only found two leaky water spigots. And those had been quick fixes. But now, we stood in the road looking at site 75. Or lake number 75, as Roy called it, since water shot out ten feet in all directions from the spigot, which was attached to a post.

"Whoa," Summer said.

I heard plastic rustling and looked over to find Packrat pulling rain ponchos out of one of his inside coat pockets. He handed me one. "Gonna need it."

I laughed. Of course we were.

Sliding the one-piece poncho over my head, I tugged it down until all the folds were smoothed out.

Packrat held out a poncho to Roy, who looked down his nose at it.

"What? I don't need one of those. I don't mind a little water."

"A little water?" Summer looked at the geyser and back at Roy, before grabbing the poncho for herself. "You'll be a drowned rat in two minutes!"

"Actually," Packrat said, "that's not a true statement. It takes a lot to drown a rat. Did you know they can tread water for five days?"

Oh, no. Here we go.

Summer glared back at Packrat. "And do you know the Bosavi woolly rat is the biggest rat in the whole, wide world?"

Rather than listen to my friends one-up each other again, I grabbed the toolbox and ran into the spray toward the water spigot, keeping my head down. My sneakers and the bottoms of my jeans got instantly soaked in the inches-deep puddle. Water sprayed from all sides of the plastic faucet like a lawn sprinkler, only faster. I tried to turn it off, but the handle just spun around and around. *That's weird.* Looking closer, I saw a crack down the side of the valve body, too.

"Wow! This one really must've frozen over the winter. Gotta replace the whole spigot," I yelled to my friends, who'd joined me under the falling water.

I loosened the clamp that held it in the water pipe. Roy wiggled the spigot with an adjustable wrench until it was loose enough to pull out.

"Get ready," he shouted. Giving it one more hard tug, he popped it out.

Water shot in all directions at first, then it poured from the pipe three feet in front of us.

"Quick!" I told Packrat, "Put in a new one!"

Packrat held it, Roy tapped it in the pipe with a mallet, and I tightened the clamp back up.

Silence.

The spray had stopped. We all cheered and jumped around in the puddles. Summer took off her poncho and grinned. "That was fun! And I'm not even that wet!"

Packrat slowly reached out to turn the handle. *POP! Whoosh!* Water rained down on us again!

"Shut it off!" I yelled to Packrat.

"Can't!" he yelled back.

The new spigot had popped off! Water dripping from my hair into my eyes and onto my nose, I looked at my friends, who'd all frozen in place. I caught Packrat's twinkling eyes, and he giggled. Roy snorted.

And there was Summer, hands clenched at her sides, her mouth an O, staring down at her sopping-wet clothes.

She'd gotten a blast of water right smack in the face!

Chapter 16

*Foxes prefer to sleep in the open, even in the winter.
Curling up, they'll wrap their tails around their bodies
and heads for warmth. Dens are only used as a nursery
for kits, or in times of horrible weather.*

"He *did* do it on purpose," Summer mumbled under her breath
for the gazillionth time. I tried to convince her Packrat hadn't; he'd just
wanted to see if the spigot worked after we'd fixed it.

At least, that's what he'd said.

With water spraying everywhere, we'd had to put on a new spigot,
because the other had shot off like a rocket from the built-up water
pressure. By the time we were done and I'd tightened that clamp with
two hands as much as I could, we were cold and wet, and Roy had
started sniffling.

So we'd headed back to my house. Summer hadn't wanted to
kayak home, so she'd called her dad and asked him to come get her.

Now, Summer was drying her hair with a towel in my kitchen, grumbling about how wet she'd gotten. She kept shooting narrow-eyed glares
toward a dry Packrat, who was pulling everything from his pockets, laying
the items on my kitchen table, so he could throw his coat in our dryer.

A knock on the door had Summer throwing the towel on a stool
as she ran to open it. Turning to us, she raised a good-bye hand as she
backed out onto my front porch.

"See ya, Cooper! I'll be back—"

"Wait a minute there, girl," her dad said, appearing behind her, his
eyes crinkling in the corners from laughter as he gently urged her back
into the kitchen. "Look at you! You weren't kidding when you said you
were soaking wet!"

Summer's dad was as tall as my own, with dark, curly hair. Pushing his black glasses up on his nose with a pointer finger, he smiled widely at me. I smiled back.

He went on, "Sorry to hear about the accident. Summer says you've really stepped up, doing what you can to get open. If there's anything I can—"

"There's nothing on the list you know how to do," Summer butted in.

Her dad frowned, and I felt a little bad for him.

Summer pulled on the ends of her wet hair as she inched toward the door. "I mean, it's all, like, hard work, and—"

Her dad's left eyebrow shot up. "Are you saying I don't work hard on—"

"*No!* No. I'm not." Another big sigh came from Summer. "I'm not saying that at all. It's a lot of outdoor work, Daddy." Her voice went soft and pleading. "Sorry."

He laughed. "No, I get what you're saying. Still," he looked right at me, as if willing me to take him seriously, "I do know how to use a shovel and a screwdriver and a hammer, and any number of other tools."

"A paintbrush?" I joked.

To my surprise, he shook his head. "I can, but you don't want me to. I'm very messy at it."

It was my turn to raise an eyebrow. Summer actually put both hands on her dad's back, pushing him toward the door. "Can we go? I'm freezing!"

"Fine!" he said, chuckling and waving good-bye as he walked down the steps to his car.

"Bye, Roy! Cooper!" Summer said in a rush. Halfway out the door, she paused, then twirled back into the kitchen. Before the screen door could slam shut behind her, she'd grabbed Roy's glass of water out of his hands to dump it on Packrat's head. "That's for turning the spigot on me. Now you're as wet as the rest of us."

And out the door she went.

Packrat's hair fell in his eyes as water dripped off his bangs.

Roy laughed and threw a towel at him. "She wins!"

"Oh, this isn't over yet," Packrat vowed. His voice faded as I thought about what I'd just heard.

A messy painter. Hmm.

Later, when we'd all taken hot showers, changed, and met back at my place, I came up with the great idea of hauling my tent out of the attic and setting it up on the front lawn. We were going to have our first campout of the season!

I was walking down the attic steps backwards with one end of the rolled-up tent, Packrat higher up on the other end facing me, and Roy behind him, holding the tarp and poles. Suddenly, Mom called out from somewhere in the store, "What are you three doing up there?"

"Nothing!" I automatically replied. But I knew that wasn't going to be the end of it.

"Cooooper!" she warned, footsteps heading our way.

"I'm getting my tent," I called back.

"Oh! Okay." Her footsteps walked away, back toward the registration counter. Packrat shifted his end of the tent, as if he were going to take another step down. I shook my head and held up five fingers. I dropped one to make four. Three.

Two.

One.

Mom's footsteps rushed back. "Your tent?" she called out, just before her head poked around the doorway to look up the stairs at us. "Isn't it a bit early in the season for that?"

"I checked the weather," I assured her. "It'll be dry out."

"It's April! It'll be cold at night."

"The end of April," I pointed out. "Our sleeping bags are rated for subzero temperatures; it's not gonna be minus one degree, is it?"

She opened her mouth. Closed it. Pointed her finger at us, and opened her mouth again. Finally she said, "I've got nothing." And she walked away.

Packrat gave me a worried look. "*Your* mom has nothing?"

"Weird," Roy agreed.

"She's tired," I said. "Works to our advantage."

But I kept thinking about it as we hauled the tent carefully through the store.

Mom *had* been really distracted lately. When Molly mentioned that we'd climbed the tower, Mom had said, "Oh, really? That's nice." And when Roy had slipped up and told her we'd driven the dump truck back to the workshop when Vern forgot it, she had said, "Nice job." It was like someone had taken my mom and replaced her with an I-don't-care-what-you-do mom.

I didn't blame her, though. I kept zoning out, too. I'd be going along, working or talking to the guys, and then *WHAM!* I'd remember that this wasn't a regular day. That Dad wasn't out in the camp working, but he was in a hospital bed. Then I'd picture him lying there, head in his hands, thinking, "If only Cooper had listened to me. If only he'd come right back from the water tower, I wouldn't have to have surgery on my arm. I'd be home with my family right now, getting ready for the *Camping with the Kings* taping."

"Cooper! Watch out!"

Packrat's yell, and his tug on the rolled-up tent, brought me back from my daydream. I'd come wicked close to knocking over a stack of ceramic loons by Mom's register, waiting to be priced and put on the store shelves.

Sigh. That's exactly what I was talking about.

While my friends got the tent set up on the lawn, I went into the house to make sandwiches and grab chips, drinks, and cookies. Arms loaded, I went back out to the tent. Packrat and Roy had the lantern going and their bags rolled out. My eyes fell to the stinky T-shirt and shoes in the middle of the tent floor.

I stopped, half in, half out of the tent.

"It's still in the baggie," Packrat reassured me.

My eyes weren't watering. No rotten smells hit my nose. I went ahead and sat down on my own sleeping bag.

Roy pointed toward the bag. "I'm telling you, it's just some kid's stinky gym clothes. Maybe someone threw them out the bus window 'cause they were stinking it up."

"One problem," I said. "That spot where we found them? Not close to the road."

"An animal dragged it there?"

"I don't think even animals would want anything to do with this."

Packrat said, "I've been thinking. Have you ever smelled a gym bag or a shoe that stunk like this?"

Roy snorted. "You go around smelling gym bags?"

"No, but I play soccer! How different can my bag be from the others?"

"What kind of smell do ya think it is?" I asked.

Packrat shrugged.

"Maybe we should compare," I suggested. "Kind of like a science experiment."

"Like how?" Roy asked.

"We'll take the smelliest sneaker here, sniff it, then open the bag quick and see if it's the same smell."

"So how do we decide which one of us has the smelliest sneakers?" Roy asked.

Packrat and I just stared at him.

"Wait a minute!" Roy cried. "Oh, fine! You can have my sneaker, but there's no way I want to sniff that shirt again!" Roy waved his hands in front of me. "I almost lost my lunch last time!"

Packrat held out a hand. "Hand one over."

"Are you sure?" Roy asked, his grin a little on the evil side as he slid off his once-white sneaker without untying it.

"Just promise that if I die, you'll donate my coat to science," Packrat said, sniffing Roy's shoe. He promptly crossed his eyes, stuck out his tongue, and fell over backwards. Roy nudged him with his foot. "Can't get up!" Packrat groaned. "I'm dying from asphyxia . . . asphyxia . . ."

"Asphyxiation?" I finished.

"Yeah, that!"

"You haven't even smelled the T-shirt!" Roy scoffed.

"Your shoe is worse. Way worse."

I burst out laughing. Roy threw a pillow at Packrat's head.

Packrat sat up, suddenly looking very serious. He lifted the giant baggie, and holding a side in one hand, put his other hand over the zipper part.

"Can't be as bad as some of the trash cans we've emptied," he said. "Right?"

For an answer, Roy and I pinched our noses.

Packrat took a deep breath, then, in one motion, unzipped the baggie, took a sniff, and zipped it up again.

I swear it was open for only two or three seconds, but the smell had Roy scrambling along the tent floor to stick his head outside into the darkness. I heard him suck in big gulps of cool air as I plunked myself down on my stomach beside him, Packrat close behind.

My eyes burned and watered. "What *is* that?" I cried. "If smells could kill, that'd be one!"

"Kitty litter," Packrat said, wiping his own eyes. "It smells like kitty litter."

"How do ya know?" I asked.

Cooper and Packrat: Mystery of the Missing Fox

"My grandma has a cat. When Mom and I go check on her, my job is to empty the litter box. It's the ammonia that's so bad."

"Who the heck soaks their shirt and shoes with cat pee?" Roy cried between gulps of air.

I backed myself into the tent. "I wonder—"

"What?" Packrat grabbed Roy's sweatshirt and tugged him in, too.

Pulling my tablet out from under my pillow, I typed the words *fox den* and *kitty litter* into the search bar.

Packrat and Roy looked over my shoulder.

"Wait. What?" Roy laughed until he fell over on his sleeping bag. "You've got to be kidding me. Like you'd ever find—"

Not taking my eyes off the little rainbow wheel of death, I grabbed Roy's pillow and threw it at his head.

Packrat leaned forward, holding his hand out to Roy. "If Cooper *does* find something useful, then *you* have to cluck like a chicken from the top of the playground climber. On Memorial Day Weekend!"

Roy sat straight up. "Good one! 'Cause when Coop doesn't find anything, there will be lots of campers to watch you cluck." He shook Packrat's hand. "You're on."

When the information came up on the screen, my two friends leaned in as I read aloud: "If you want to get rid of foxes who are denning near your house, a humane way is to put pee-soaked kitty litter, or a sweaty T-shirt, socks, or sneakers, in or near the den opening."

"Darn it!" Roy threw his pillow back at Packrat. Packrat punched the pillow, put it on top of his own, then lay on both of them with his arms behind his head. Roy tugged his pillow out and, punching it back to the way he liked it, climbed into his own sleeping bag. The minute he was in, he yawned.

"Another clue," Packrat said, echoing Roy's yawn with one of his own.

I bookmarked the website, put the tablet away, and crawled into my bag, too.

"We're ahead of schedule with the chores; maybe we could go back to the den tomorrow. Make sure our mysterious fox hater didn't put anything else there."

"What do you mean, mysterious?" Roy scoffed. "It's Cat Lady. No doubt about it. She was walking around the woods right before we found the stinky bundle. She could have taken the trail cam, easy. And she has cats. Duh."

Packrat yawned again. "I still think it's Summer and her dad. Sorry, Coop." He rolled onto one side to see me. "Summer could have left that T-shirt just as easily as Cat Lady. She kayaks over here and walks your trails like she owns the place, without you! She's always giving us animal facts. She knows when we're working every day, and when we'll be at the blind."

I opened my mouth to protest, but he kept on.

"She said her dad's a painter. He says he can't paint."

"No." I snuggled deeper into my own sleeping bag, so I didn't have to look at him for fear he'd see how frustrated I was. Why wouldn't he stop picking on Summer?

"She *said* he's an artist. And what's that got to do with—"

"She won't say what kind," Packrat insisted. He lowered his voice. "I think he's into something she doesn't want us to know about. The warden pulled her aside, remember? So it's something to do with animals or nature or wildlife laws!" He flopped back down on his pillow.

Roy put out the lamp, and his sleepy voice drifted through the darkened tent. "What about the missing kit? You think someone got it, Cooper?"

I paused. Those clothes didn't get there by themselves. The trail camera didn't walk away on its own. But Summer having anything to do with it? I just couldn't wrap my mind around that.

The loons called then, a low, haunting call. One sounded as if it was at one end of the lake, the other, halfway across.

"Wonder if they're nesting," I said, glad of the distraction so I didn't have to answer Roy's question. As it turned out, I didn't have to answer it anyhow. They were both breathing heavily, already asleep. I looked at my watch. Nine-thirty.

Normally when we camp out, we're up so late, Mom or Dad has to come out and shush us, then threaten us with sleeping inside. My friends were the best, putting in all these working hours for me. For my family.

As I fell asleep, I thought, *There's got to be a good explanation. I just have to find it . . .*

I am running through the woods. I look over my shoulder to see the black coyote closing in fast, fangs bared, eyes bright. I race through the woods, pushing branches out of my way, not caring if they scratch my arms and legs. Not caring if they snap back. With any luck, their sharp tips will poke out the eyes of the beast.

All I can think of is getting home. Back to Dad. He'll help me! I try to yell, but no sound comes from my mouth.

I hear heavy breathing, smell the stench of its breath over my shoulder. It's getting closer.

I race through the campground gate and round the corner to Raccoon Trail. The fallen tree! It's blocking my way!

Maaaaaaaah! Maaaaaaaah!

The fox? Calling! It's all right! But I can't lead the coyote to it.

"Cooper?"

Who is it? Dad? Dad! Under the tree! I'm leading the coyote right to him! No!

Maaaaaaaah! Maaaaaaaah!

"Cooper? Cooper!"

Dad! Get away! Run! I try to yell, but the words won't come out. *Run!!*

"Cooper!"

I awoke with a start. Packrat. He put a finger to his lips and whispered, "Cooper? Get up! I think I heard something!"

Chapter 17

Foxes can run for miles if need be.

Maaaaaaaah! Maaaaaaaah!

The fox.

"Cooper!" Packrat shook my shoulder again. "Right outside!"

Roy sat up to pull his sweatshirt over his head.

I was confused. "The fox?"

"No. Before that! I swear I heard footsteps right outside the tent."

I slid out of my sleeping bag, grabbing my sneakers from the end of it.

"So? People walk by the front yard all the—"

"No, *right* outside! And they stopped. Like they were listening to us."

Roy froze. "How long ago?"

"Twenty minutes. I almost looked out, but whoever it was walked away after, like, I don't know, it felt like five, ten minutes." Packrat slid one arm, then the other into his jacket. "Thought my imagination was running away with me."

Roy crawled over to unzip the tent flap. "You think they were checking to see if we were asleep?" he asked Packrat.

Maaaaaaaah!

He nodded grimly. "Now I do. Yeah."

I followed Roy out, Packrat behind me. "If you're right, they're out there now." I looked at my friends and said, "Let's go catch a fox hater."

Packrat handed me a small red flashlight, although I didn't really need it. The almost-full moon shone down through the trees like a giant lantern. It was kind of cool how the forest was all lit up yet there were deep, dark shadows everywhere, too. Roy, Packrat, and I jogged out the campground gate area, down the driveway, and onto the red-blazed trail.

Maaaaaaaah!

We stopped.

Maaaaaaaah!

I turned toward the sound, which was much, much fainter now, and muffled, too. It seemed to be farther up the trail. We picked up the pace again, trying to hurry, but without making too much noise.

When we reached the fork in the trail, we stopped again. All we could hear was our own heavy breathing. No more fox call. No footsteps.

"We're too late," I said quietly.

"Maybe it's not what we thought," Packrat suggested. But I could tell he wasn't convinced of that.

"Let's go check anyway," I said. "Maybe the mother fox was just spooked or something."

Choosing our steps very carefully now, we moved toward the blind. Once there, Roy looked inside it. "It's clear," he said, slipping in. Packrat and I followed.

Through the screen window, I stared at the fox den. Luckily, no tree shadows crossed the opening, and the moonlight shone a pure white light on it. I couldn't see inside it, though. That was pitch-black. Were the kits in its shadow, spying on us? I lifted my flashlight, waffling on whether or not to use it, when Packrat nudged my shoulder with something. His night-vision binoculars! I grinned a *Thank you* at him before raising them to my eyes.

The woods were silent, which wasn't a surprise, considering we thought someone had been here, harassing the foxes. We were silent, too, hoping the kits would come out so we could take a head count.

Slowly, the middle-of-the-night woodland creatures started moving again. A scurry through the leaves to our left. A frog croak in the distance, and an answer from our right. Raccoons moving around on a branch overhead, as insects made high, squeaky buzzing sounds all around us.

The fox den remained quiet.

Suddenly, something flew between us and the den with a wing-span so large, I ducked a little, even though I was inside the blind. *Hoo-HOO-hoo-hoo!* Landing on the branch of a dead pine tree, the owl stared down at us, before turning its head 180 degrees. Recognizing the two ear-like tufts on either side of its head, I gasped.

"A great horned owl!" I whispered.

There was something wiggling in its talons. A mouse, perhaps.

Roy pointed to the den. I swung the night-vision binoculars that way to find shiny eyes peering out. Three sets only. My heart sank. One of the kits stepped out to sit on the ledge. Two more followed. They seemed upset, whining and pacing. There was no pouncing or wrestling or tumbling. Only worried gazes into the woods.

Could we really have lost two kits already?

The owl took flight and the kits scampered back into the den. Again, I searched for the mother fox. Maybe she had the other kits with her? Did they get caught outside?

Nothing.

Wait. What was that? I played with the focus on the binoculars. I wasn't seeing things! There! In a bush. A glint of light on metal, halfway from the blind to the den.

My friends and I left the blind, working our way to the tall, thick bushes until we found the piece of metal that had reflected the moon-light. Hanging off a branch in the thickest part of the bush was a wide U-shaped handle. The ends looked odd, like it'd been ripped off of something. Not dirty or rusty, though. Newish-looking. Where had it come from?

"Looks like you weren't imagining things, Packrat," Roy whispered.

I agreed. "We need to figure out what's happening to the kits, and fast."

Chapter 18

A female fox will not hesitate to move her kits if she feels the den is threatened in any way.

The next morning, I sat up and grabbed my sweatshirt before heading out into the cool, damp, spring air. The handle we'd found last night fell from the pocket.

I picked it up to study it. Silver and shiny, almost brand-new. It looked like it was supposed to be in a wider U shape, but one of the ends had been broken off and straightened. The other was slightly twisted. It hadn't been by the den yesterday morning, or the day I'd checked the trail cam. Where had it come from?

I had to get back there. Everything in me screamed that those kits were in serious trouble. First, the male fox in the trap. Then the smelly T-shirt and sneakers, and the trail cam missing. And we hadn't seen all five fox kits in days! When I'd first thought someone was just trying to scare the foxes away, that was one thing. But this handle? That brought to mind worse things. Much worse.

Could it be from a trap? Was a poacher hanging around there? The same one who had trapped the male fox?

Or was my imagination running away with me? With us? I knew nature, and the odds of all five fox kits surviving the summer weren't good.

I turned the handle over in my hands. No, something was going on, and I was willing to bet it wasn't nature at work.

I shook the lump that was Packrat. As usual, he only burrowed deeper into his camouflage-colored sleeping bag. Roy sat up, rubbing his head with his hands. I nudged Packrat again.

"I could blow a whistle," Roy suggested. "Right into the bag."

He leaned over to get Packrat's coat, knowing, like I did, that there was bound to be a whistle in there somewhere.

But I had a better idea. I reached outside the tent to bring in the giant baggie. The one with the stinky T-shirt and sneakers.

"You wouldn't!" Roy whispered, but his eyes lit up and his lips curved upward.

I hesitated. Then I smiled.

As I cracked open the baggie, I pulled my sweatshirt up over my nose, then, with my thumb and pointer finger, carefully took out one of the super-stinky sneakers.

Roy pulled his sweatshirt up over his nose, too, then held up all ten fingers.

"He's out by five," he bet, his voice muffled. "And if I win, *you* have to cluck like a chicken from the top of the climber on Memorial Day Weekend. In a chicken suit!"

"By seven," I insisted, cringing at the thought of clucking like a chicken, in a chicken suit, on one of our busiest camping weekends. I opened the end of Packrat's sleeping bag and tossed the sneaker in. "You're on."

One. Two. Packrat stirred.

Three. Four. The sleeping bag wiggled.

Five. Arms and legs punched from inside the bag, in all directions.

"The smell!" his voice cried. "I'm dying!"

Then nothing. No movement.

"Did we kill him?" Roy joked.

Six. Seven. The sneaker flew from the bag, right before Packrat's head popped out to gasp for breath.

"That's gross!" he cried. "Mean!"

The sneaker landed in Roy's lap, making his sweatshirt fall off his nose. He started to open his mouth to yell, then clamped it shut and held his breath as he lifted the sneaker with two fingers and tossed it outside the tent.

Gulping fresh air, Roy blinked several times, tears forming in the corners of his eyes.

"What the heck?" he cried.

"Serves you right!" Packrat wiped his eyes, too. "That is the nastiest smell ever! No wonder it can make foxes move."

The foxes! I pulled out the handle so we could all look at it again. Neither one of my friends could figure out what it was either. Roy immediately thought of Cat Lady's cat carrier, but Packrat pointed out that it had been plastic. At least, he thought so.

We'd have to find out.

We crawled from the tent to find a drizzly, rainy kind of day. But it smelled good, clean-like, especially after that sneaker! I found it on the ground, shoved it back in the plastic bag with the rest of the stinky stuff, sealed the bag, and tossed it in the tent for safekeeping.

Roy barked, "Are you crazy? It'll never smell the same in there again!"

He reached in and snatched the bag off the tent floor to toss it back to me.

He was right. We had a whole summer ahead of us, and I didn't want to be smelling that smell every time we camped out. "Then where?" I asked.

Packrat pulled another big baggie from his coat.

"We'll double-bag it," he said, slipping the first one into the second and sealing it tight. Then he put the whole thing in a large inner pocket.

I raised an eyebrow.

"It's a clue," he said with a shrug.

I wasn't sure I trusted the double-bag system, but, hey, I wasn't the one wearing the coat.

We crossed over to the still-darkened store, about half an hour before it was supposed to open. Normally Mom would be out here, bringing in the morning newspapers and making pots of coffee for the customers, but I knew she was probably on the phone with Dad, saying good morning and asking about the surgery on his arm today.

Just as my key touched the keyhole, the door swung open a couple of inches.

"That's weird," I mumbled. I slowly pushed the door open a little more. "Mom? Mom?"

The lights weren't on. The papers were still rolled in a bundle on the porch. Yet there were smudged, muddy footprints crossing the floor.

"What the heck?" Roy spat out.

I turned to find him feeling the doorjamb, where the door clicks shut. He looked like he wanted to take someone down.

"There's marks here. Someone jimmied the door open."

"What? No way!"

Who'd break into our store? I mean, we didn't even have any business yet.

I rushed over to the cash register, but the stacks of ones, fives, and ten-dollar bills Mom had left in it overnight were still there. It didn't look like anything was missing. I mean, I wouldn't know if twenty bucks or one bag of chips had walked away or something, or even a sweatshirt, but the cash register and shelves were far from empty.

Roy checked the back room while Packrat checked Mom's office. The three of us met back by the registration counter, shrugging our shoulders.

Packrat ran a hand over his head a couple times. "That's so weird!"

Roy nodded. "I know! Maybe the marks were on the door before and we never noticed them? Maybe your mom didn't shut the door tight? Who'd go to all the work of breaking in and then not take anything?"

"Doesn't make sense," I agreed.

Packrat moved toward the coffee counter. "I can't think! I haven't had my hot cocoa yet!"

I went with him, still looking around the darkened store, hoping to find a clue.

We'd just taken our first deep sips of hot chocolate a few minutes later when we heard, "Anyone in there?"

The man's voice had me bobbling my hot cocoa, making it drip over the sides and onto my hands.

"Ow!" I cried, putting a burnt knuckle in my mouth. Grumpy that we'd found the store broken into, and now I'd burned my hand, I called back, "We aren't open yet! It'll be a minute!"

"Ice-cream delivery," the man called back.

I swear my friends have never moved so fast, not even when we were being chased by some goons who were trying to steal an eaglet last summer.

Packrat opened the front door wide and threw the lights on, while Roy showed the ice-cream man the way to the freezer.

"Sorry to hear about your dad," he said, stopping in front of me to hand me the bill. He asked gently, "How's he doing?"

"He's getting better," I said.

"And the campground? You'll be okay to open?" His kind eyes met mine.

"I think so . . ." I hesitated.

Cat Lady came to the door, a bright pink umbrella over her head, and butted right in to our conversation.

"You have a major water leak; there's water spraying everywhere! Water pressure in my camper is really low. It took seven whole minutes to fill the cats' water dish!"

"Oh, the poor cats," Roy muttered behind me.

"What did you say?" Cat Lady's head whipped around.

Roy cleared his throat when I shot him a be-nice-to-the-customer look. "I said, 'We'll take care of that.' "

"Oh." Her face softened. "Thank you."

"What site?" I asked.

"Twenty-two," she said, turning to leave. Then she turned back.

"And when you see Vern, would you tell him to keep his raven on his own site? That crazy bird keeps coming on mine to eat my cats' food."

I sighed as the bobbing pink umbrella crossed paths with Mom. Since she was on her way over, I knew the ice-cream delivery man would be taken care of.

"Packrat, get our hot cocoas. Roy, can you grab the golf cart and the water tools again? Meet you guys out front."

I walked into Mom's office and grabbed my radio off the shelf. Then I reached up for my maintenance keys to pull them off the hook with my name on it. Turning, I walked out of Mom's office.

Halfway across the store I stopped.

And I went back.

The hook with Dad's name was empty. No keys.

That's what the robber had come for.

Chapter 19

Foxes have been known to leave droppings on an uncovered trap, almost as if they're letting the trapper know they'd found it, or perhaps as a warning for other foxes.

"Maybe I didn't shut the door tight behind me last night," Mom said. "And it rained, so those footprints could have happened then. They could be mine!" She sighed. "I've been so forgetful lately, what with your dad's surgery today and getting this place ready for the *Camping with the Kings* people. I bet I misplaced your father's keys. Vern handed them to me after he used the dump truck yesterday. And I kind of recall hanging them up."

"Kind of?" I pressed.

"Summer and her dad had just come in to say good-bye and Bo was flying around in here, checking everything out. Why I don't ask him to leave—" She stopped and gave a half-smile. "Oh! Who am I kidding? I have a soft spot for that bird. At any rate, nothing else is missing. I think the keys are just misplaced."

The ice-cream man called from where he was stocking the freezer, saying, "If I had a nickel for every time I've misplaced mine . . ."

"Call the police!" I begged her, ignoring him.

"I'm not calling them, Cooper, just because a set of keys is missing. Money from the register, stock from the store, your father's tools—of course I'd call. But just a set of keys?" She waved it off. "I'll check with Vern when he gets back from his doctor's appointment in town. He might remember what I did with them."

Packrat, Roy, and I were pretty sure that Mom hadn't misplaced them, but we couldn't convince her. When she walked over to check in with the ice-cream man, Packrat knelt on the floor and pulled out a measuring tape, a notebook, and a pencil. Roy sketched the footprint while Packrat read off the measurements.

"The sneakers!" I whispered.

Packrat took out the baggie and opened it up to tug out one of the sneakers. Roy and I pinched our noses again. I shuddered. Would that smell ever go away? Packrat held it up against the muddy footprint. I looked from Packrat to Roy and back at the sneaker next to the print. The sneaker was definitely smaller, by about two sizes.

"Do you smell something?" I heard Mom ask the ice-cream man.

Packrat quickly stuffed the sneaker back in the bag and closed it up tight before putting it in his coat.

"We'll fix that leak on site twenty-two, Mom!" I called as we slipped out the front door.

"Wait! Cooper?"

I stopped on the porch, my friends going ahead to get the tools we'd need. Mom joined me.

"Aren't you coming with me and Molly to see Dad today?"

I hesitated, at war with myself. I wanted to go, but it still made me feel weird and guilty and stuff when I saw him all banged up. The fox kits needed me, too. And I wanted to get the campground ready so Dad wouldn't have so much to do when he got home.

I think Mom saw the almost-answer on my face, because her eyes got kinda sad. I quickly said, "Let me see how bad this leak is, okay?"

She nodded, biting her lip. "Cooper? I really worry that—"

My eyes started to sting and my stomach did flips.

"Don't worry," I said, walking backward. I hadn't just hurt Dad, I'd hurt Mom, too. She had too much to do without him here. "I know the *Camping with the Kings* crew will arrive in two days, but the guys and me, we'll fix the leak. And get the rest of the stuff done, too. You just help, Dad. I got it. Honest."

Cooper and Packrat: Mystery of the Missing Fox

It wasn't hard to find the split line. Not when the Wilder Family Campground Geyser could be seen three sites away. Packrat just had to name it.

The three of us stood on the edge of the site, watching water shoot six feet up in the air, before falling in a mud puddle. I shook my head. "Wasn't planning on taking a shower again today."

Roy scoffed. "Do you ever?"

I shoved him. "Twice as often as you!"

Roy shoved me back.

Packrat kept staring at the geyser. "Could be worse."

Roy and I stopped shoving long enough to look his way.

"Could be a toilet geyser."

Roy and I burst out laughing.

Packrat took out the ponchos while I got the clamps and other tools we'd need to replace this section of hose.

Then we went in.

Thirty minutes later, our sneakers were soaking wet, but the ponchos had kept the rest of us pretty dry. We stood back to look proudly on our job well done.

We'd just put all the tools back on the golf cart when Packrat's mom came over the radio.

"Hey, boys—done with that leak yet?"

"Yep," I answered, grinning at my friends.

"I hate to tell you, but there's another. Not as big, but it's still gushing. Mrs. Nichols found it on her way to the lake. Site fifty-five."

"We're on it," I said, climbing into the driver's seat. Packrat sat on the back of the cart, while Roy hopped in beside me with the toolbox.

This time, the leak was more like a dribbler, compared to the last one. But it was bad enough to create some runoff at the back of the site, so we figured we should rake and fix that, too.

The three of us stood side by side. "We'll take care of it, and then tackle the clues," I assured Roy and Packrat.

After, we went back to Packrat's camper for some of his amazing grilled cheese sandwiches. His secret: three kinds of cheese between two slices of homemade bread, placed in a sandwich basket that he held over campfire coals. We didn't have time to build a fire today, so we just used his camp stove. It was just as good. I'd just taken my first bite into a steamy, oozing, gooey sandwich when my radio crackled.

"Cooper?"

I sighed, not wanting to put my sandwich down.

"What's up?"

Seeing Roy's hand inching toward my sandwich, I made a fist and tried to pound it. I missed.

"Water leak on site one-oh-two," Packrat's mom replied. "I saw it on my way back to the store from lunch."

"What? But—" I let go of the button to say to my friends, "You got to be kidding me!" Aiming for Roy's hand, and hitting it this time, I picked up my sandwich and told her, "We're on it."

After that, a leak popped up on site 95. And site 4.

"What the heck!" Roy said every time someone called in a new report. Packrat only shook his head.

When we finished, the sun was dropping fast. And so were we. Had we done something wrong when we turned on the water? I couldn't remember Dad having so many water leaks in one day. And there was the spigot, too. But then again, I was usually at school when he did this getting-ready-to-open stuff. No wonder he always snored in his chair after suppertime.

Done for the day, Packrat, Roy, and I slowly walked into the store. I grabbed a bottle of water, Roy grabbed a Coke, and Packrat a chocolate milk before slumping into a chair in the coffee area. Mom came over.

"I heard you had a tough day, boys," she said, placing two large take-out pizza boxes in the middle of the table.

I was so tired, I couldn't even reach across the table for a slice. Roy, on the other hand, threw open a cover, slid a piece of Meat Lover's Pizza onto a plate, and practically swallowed it whole before Packrat could take his own slice.

Mom pulled out a chair to sit next to me and put a slice onto a paper plate for me.

"I have two pieces of good news: One, the surgery on your dad's arm went so well, they're sending him home tomorrow!" She tipped her head to one side to catch my eye, hers filling with tears. "I'll feel so much better when he's here. Home, with us. Won't you?"

I smiled and nodded, but my eyes looked everywhere except at her. I wanted him home, too, but fixing all those water lines had kept us from opening the bathrooms today. We were behind schedule now, and I still had my promise to keep.

"And two," Mom continued, "I found Dad's keys! Well, Vern did. He said he found them outside the back door here. I must have taken them from him and then dropped them." She leaned across the table to put her hand on mine. "See? It all worked out."

I'd wanted the guys to stay over again, but Mom gently told Packrat and Roy to sleep in Packrat's camper, saying, "All three of you are asleep on your feet from fixing those lines today. What you need is a solid night's rest. Don't come to work until ten a.m. tomorrow. That's an order."

When I'd protested starting so late, with so much to do, she'd shushed me.

"Even your dad understands the need for a little extra sleep, Cooper."

In the house, I found Molly in her pajamas, watching a DVD about a unicorn and a fairy trying to save a rainbow from losing all its colors.

"Cooper!" She jumped up to hug me tight around the waist, then dragged me to the couch. "Watch with me? It's just at the good part!"

"For a minute." Fairies and unicorns weren't my thing. Rainbows, either. But I was too tired to say no.

Molly snuggled up beside me. Her soft voice, reciting all the fairy's lines word for word, even the songs, had my eyes drooping. The next thing I knew, I woke up on the couch, covered with a blanket, smelling hot cocoa. I turned to find a steaming cup on the coffee table next to me.

I stretched and rubbed my eyes.

"There you are, sleepyhead!" Mom stepped around the corner. "I know I told you to sleep late, but when I covered you with blankets last night, you made me promise to wake you at seven. Something about being worried about the little foxes?"

I sat the rest of the way up, suddenly awake. "I think they're in trouble."

Mom put the hot mug of cocoa in my hands and kissed the top of my head.

"Go. But come back for ten a.m., okay? Molly and I are going in to get Dad. Bring him home. We'd like you to come with us."

I sipped my cocoa. Stalling for time. How to tell her?

"Mom, I have to help the guys super-clean the bathrooms to get them open. They're getting here at ten, remember? And the television crew shows up tomorrow. I think I should stay."

Mom frowned as she sat on the coffee table next to me.

"Roy and Packrat have cleaned them before; couldn't they manage without you?"

I shrugged. "Opening the bathrooms is different. There's certain stuff you do when you open-clean that you don't do when you're just regular-cleaning them."

Mom tucked a loose strand of hair behind her ear, staring at me in that I-know-you're-not-telling-me-everything way she has.

"I just"—Mom's voice cracked, as she cleared her throat—"I just wanted us all to be together as a family."

I nodded. I wanted that, too, but I figured I had to put things back the way they were supposed to be first. I couldn't fix Dad's arm, or the bruise on his head, but I could fix the campground. I could have it ready for the *Camping with the Kings* show and all its fans. And when the calls to camp started coming in like crazy, then maybe he'd forgive me.

And not in a dads-have-to-forgive-their-sons way, either.

All the way.

Chapter 20

Being shy animals, foxes tend to hunt mostly in the twilight hours, and at night. If you see one hunting during the day, it could mean it's putting in extra hours to feed its kits.

I sat in the blind, eating the granola bar I'd grabbed on my way out the door. I'd left the house so fast, I hadn't even brought my backpack with me. Without binoculars, I couldn't tell if the mother fox was around or not. No new dirt had been thrown outside the den—no new food that I could see.

"Sorry I wasn't here yesterday," I whispered.

Yesterday. What a disaster. A whole day spent fixing water-line leaks. What had I done wrong? Did I open the valves too quickly? Should I have waited to open the valve to the water tower? It was a day we should have spent cleaning the bathrooms and raking sites, while the chlorine set in the lines and disinfected them. I could have brought boats to the lake. Or planted flowers. Could we still get it all done by noon tomorrow?

One little reddish face appeared in the den opening. In spite of the worry in the pit of my stomach, I felt the sides of my mouth curling upward.

"There you are," I whispered.

A second face appeared above the first. This one whined, and ducked back inside. A few seconds later, it appeared again. Was that a third? Or was the second kit coming back again?

I sighed. There was no exact way to tell how many there were. Not without going inside the den.

If only the trail cam hadn't gone missing!

Cooper and Packrat: Mystery of the Missing Fox

The braver kit stepped out. Its ears twitched. It looked right at the blind, at me. Maybe the breeze was just right or something. It raised its head to peek over branches, then lowered it to look under, before it curled up on the shelf in the sun. Lifting a hind paw, it scratched behind an ear, then rested its chin on its front legs and closed its eyes. Less than a minute later, the second kit pounced, landing on the back of the first, and they rolled around, nipping each other's ears and chins. It was all I could do to not laugh out loud. It reminded me a little of Molly, when she wanted to wrestle.

After beating its smaller sibling, the larger kit trotted to the bottom of the bank and halfway crawled under a fallen tree trunk. It dug with its front paws until it dragged out something small and furry in its mouth.

"Rat," I whispered, seeing the kit bat the rat around with its paws. "That must be the cache of food."

The kit carried the rat in its mouth up to the shelf by the den. Lying down, it began to gnaw like crazy on it.

The smaller kit got low on its belly. Slowly, slowly, it crawled toward the kit with the rat. Pausing, it wiggled its butt and . . . pounced! The two kits went tumbling down the bank, one over the other.

Two. There were only two. If there were any other kits in the den, they would have come out by now, with that dead rat up on the shelf by itself.

I took the metal handle out of my pocket and frowned. What did it mean? What had it come from?

We'd seen no more snares like the one that had trapped the male. But somebody had been down here—and more than once, too. Were they trying to get the kits to move, or were they just watching them, like we were? And if so, why? I got that some people were afraid of bears. I wouldn't want to run into a bear in the woods, either. Or a wolf. Or even a coyote. But a fox? They caused trouble sometimes, especially if you had chickens. Or if they lived under your porch or workshop. But this den was way back in the woods. And foxes didn't even come near the campground once we were open and people came to camp. Hardly anyone even knew they were here.

Except for Cat Lady. And Vern. And Warden Kate.

And Summer.

Suddenly, the kits stood frozen at attention, ears upright and turned in the same direction: down the trail. They crouched low to watch through the branches.

Crunch, crunch.

Footsteps on leaves. Packrat and Roy must have tracked me down.

Wait. A flash of yellow? It was Summer. She looked my way, sending me a small smile to let me know she'd spotted me.

"I thought you'd be getting ready to work," she whispered, coming through the blind flap.

I looked at my watch. "I have to go in a couple of minutes. We're opening the bathrooms today."

Summer stared at the fox den.

"Sorry I couldn't help you yesterday. I wanted to. But I had some calls, and stuff to do. And Dad needed my help with his . . . latest project. Hey . . ." She looked at me. "Where's the trail camera?"

With everything that had been going on, I realized I hadn't yet told Summer about the missing trail cam. When I filled her in, her face clouded.

"How many kits are left?" she whispered.

"Two."

She sighed heavily. "I was afraid of that."

I looked at her. *Afraid of that?*

"You don't seem surprised."

She closed her eyes. "Can I ask you something? And I don't want you to freak out." She got quiet for a minute, then she leaned over to grab my sneaker and stare at me with pleading eyes. "Can we take the kits? Keep them safe. We can raise them. I saw online—"

"What? No!" I couldn't believe she'd ask me this. "Warden Kate would never allow that!"

"We won't tell her."

I ran a hand through my hair. "Summer, you can't just take these kits! We have no proof yet that they were abandoned. It hasn't been long enough."

"C'mon! Do you really think the mother is still around?"

I hitched a thumb over my shoulder toward the den. "They do! They haven't left the den yet to look for food. They look fine. We'll keep tabs on them. And I promise we'll report it to the warden. Let her know it might be a prob—"

"I knew you wouldn't understand," she said, her eyes sparking in anger like a fire being poked. "I knew you'd freak out."

"That's not fair! You know I want to be a warden someday. I have to think like one now."

Summer either didn't hear me, or didn't want to. She stood up, brushed off her pants, then reached for the tent zipper, muttering to herself, "They'll be safe with me! Safer than they are with you!"

I jumped up to follow her out of the blind. "What did you say?"

Summer turned. "If you won't do something about it, I will!" She stormed away.

Taking two steps toward her, I yelled, "No! You won't. This is my land!"

At that, she stopped to look back at me, eyes wide.

I pointed my finger at her. "My foxes!" I warned. "And we're letting nature take its course. Warden Kate would be mad if you interfered. And I'd tell her."

Summer's eyes filled with tears. She stalked a couple of yards away before turning back for a third time.

"Think about it, Cooper Wilder! You'll see that I'm right!"

Chapter 21

Foxes have many small caches of food hidden throughout their territory. That way, if one is discovered and raided by a neighboring fox, they won't lose their entire supply of food.

With every step I took along the red-blazed trail back to the campground, my head began to hurt from all the thinking I was doing. Was Summer right?

On the one hand, taking those kits now would make Warden Kate disappointed in me. Especially if they weren't really abandoned or in danger.

On the other hand, leaving them there might mean we would lose them all.

If it had been a normal spring, I would have staked out the den 24/7, waiting for proof one way or the other. But I had made a promise—to my parents and myself—to get the campground open. We had bathrooms to super clean and spigots to open so the bleached water could run out. A whole campground to rake. Maybe I should put Packrat and Roy in the blind.

No, I thought, kicking a rock, and watching as it skipped ahead of me. I couldn't get all the jobs done on my own, and Mom had to go get Dad today to bring him home. Watching the kits instead of helping Dad was what had gotten my family into this mess in the first place. I couldn't make that mistake again.

Molly greeted me at the door of the store. "Cooper! What'd you see?"

Without thinking, I said, "Nothin'."

Her face fell. "No baby foxes?"

"Kits, Molly. They're called kits."

"Sorry."

Mom frowned at me over the registration counter. She was on the phone; otherwise I might have gotten more than just a look. She said into the phone, "Yes, we have to move you to site thirty-four, if that's okay." She nodded at something the person on the other end of the line said. Soothingly, she added, "I know it's not your favorite site, but circumstances have—" She paused, bit her lip, and started again. "Ted, listen." She sighed. "I'll be honest here. My husband has been hurt. There's a chance we might not even get the park open in time."

More nodding from Mom. She looked at the ceiling as she tapped her pencil on the counter.

"Thank you. He'll be okay. He comes home today."

A pause while she listened. "Oh, I *do* think you'll like thirty-four. It has sewer, and it's bigger."

Another look at the ceiling and a bite of her lip.

"No, it's not that—yes, the power and water will be on, but what we're struggling with now is whether or not we'll have time to rake the roads and playground and such."

Mom tipped her head to one side and stared out the window. "Well, I—"

More listening. "Okay. Thank you. If you're willing to rake your own site, I have no problem with that. Thank you, Ted; I wish all my customers were as understanding as you are. Yes, I'll give Jim your best."

Mom gave me a thumbs-up as she kept talking to the customer.

I rubbed Molly's head, kind of in a sorry-I'm-so-grumpy-it's-not-you kinda way.

"Tell Vern I've already started at the bathrooms, okay?"

Molly beamed up at me. "We're going to get Daddy after this call. You comin'?"

I shook my head. "I'll see him when he gets home, okay?"

Molly frowned and reached for my hand. "Please?"

I shook my head. "You heard Mom. There's lots to do if we're going to open the campground on time for the TV cameras."

I reached for the store door. Feeling a tug on my shirt, I looked back down at Molly.

"Were the kits really all gone?" she whispered, her brow furrowed.

"No, Squirt. I saw two today."

"Oh. Only two?"

"Only two."

Super-cleaning the bathrooms from the ceiling to the floor only took half as long as I thought it would. But, as Packrat pointed out, that's probably because there weren't a lot of women here to keep us from getting in the ladies' room. We'd scrubbed toilets, sinks, showers, shower curtains, mirrors, trash cans, floors, and even the pipes where the water fed into the sinks.

Then, when every toilet stall had toilet paper and every paper towel holder was stocked, we put our cleaning supplies away and headed for the office to check the to-do list.

With my two friends on either side of me, my grumpy mood had disappeared in no time.

"Where'd you go this morning?" Roy asked. "Molly said you went for a walk."

"To the fox den," I admitted.

"What'd you see?" Roy asked.

"Only two kits."

"Two?" Roy and Packrat said at the same time.

"I know," I said, "but maybe the third just didn't come out." It was so hard to know! I hesitated before adding, "And I saw Summer."

Packrat stopped dead in the middle of the road. Roy and I turned back to look at him.

"What'd she want?"

I shrugged. "To see the kits."

Packrat muttered, "On the trail without you. Again."

"You do that, too," I pointed out.

"I stay here all summer in my camper. She doesn't." Packrat's voice, the look in his eyes, had my grumpy mood racing back.

"I know what you think of her, but she's my friend," I said, whirling around to continue down the street. "I wish you'd both just get along."

"I don't trust her." Packrat took double steps to catch up. "She's keeping secrets."

Suddenly, Roy put up a hand. He bent over low and moved to the side of the road behind some trash cans. Packrat and I gave each other what-the-heck looks before we followed.

"What?" I whispered.

Roy pointed toward Cat Lady's site. I looked, but I didn't see anything new. "So?"

"Cat carriers! Four!" he whispered, pointing to the carriers, all lined up in a row on the deck by her front door.

"We knew she had one," Packrat grumbled. "Should've known she'd have one for each cat."

"But we haven't compared the handles yet," Roy said.

I hit my hand to my forehead. Why hadn't I thought of that? I glanced at Packrat. Because I'd been too busy fighting with my best friend, that's why.

Packrat looked up and down the street. "I don't see her. Now's as good a time as any."

I nodded. One after the other, we crossed the street to crouch behind her car. I peeked around it to look down the front side of her camper, into the campsite. No one was there. I waved my friends on, over to the carriers.

They were your regular, tan, plastic carriers, with long rectangular slats in them for the cats to see out. The front doors and the latches to open and close the fronts were metal, giving me hope. But the handles on the tops of the carriers were dark brown. And plastic.

Darn it.

Vern walked around the front of the camper. "What are you three doing here?"

I jumped a mile, I swear. Before I could answer, Cat Lady came to the door and stepped out onto her deck, a dish towel in her hands.

"Did you find Fred?" She smiled at me, her face all hopeful-like.

I quickly shook my head. "No."

"That's why we're here," Packrat said. "We wanted to know if you'd seen—"

"No. My other three cats are pouting and sulking. I've searched everywhere. The woods. The campground." She sighed heavily. "I don't want to give up hope, but . . ."

"I've heard of cats missing for months, but still finding their way home," Packrat offered. "Maybe Fred accidentally got into someone's motorhome, and they accidentally drove out with him?"

"Or a car?" I added.

Cat Lady's eyes narrowed. I took a step back, thinking the look was for me, but then I realized her eyes were focused on something behind us. I turned to find Bo on the ground, his beak in a cat dish.

"Shoo!" she cried, waving her dish towel. "Shoo!" To Vern, she added, "I told you! He's eating all the food!"

I almost laughed out loud at that, because Bo only had one round piece of cat food in his beak. He looked calmly at us, then took to the sky.

"I'm so sorry," Vern said. "Perhaps you should take the food in. It could attract all kinds of animals."

Cat Lady harrumphed before turning toward her camper. She stopped, then turned toward the cat carriers. Opening one up, she put the cat food in it. She gave Vern a so-there look.

"That fox caught my Fred, I just know it! So now I'm going to catch *it*—and maybe your raven, too!"

She spun on her heel, went into the trailer, and slammed the door shut behind her.

We all just looked at each other, not quite knowing what to do.

Vern waved us back over to the road and we all walked together toward the office.

"I took care of the outside sinks; they're all leak-free and clean." Vern looked at his watch. "I'm going to break for a late lunch, then head into town for some supplies. What's your next project?"

"I think raking, but we're headed to the office to check the list and see what we can get done before supper."

Vern smiled. "And I hear your dad's coming home! Make some time for him, too."

"He'll need rest," I said quickly. "I might go see the foxes."

Vern smiled, but it didn't quite reach his eyes this time.

"Make time for your dad, Cooper. Tell him about all the hard work you've been doing. He'll be proud! The foxes will be there tomorrow. And speaking of tomorrow, I'll see you then, right? Eight o'clock?"

At my nod, he turned off to the left, to his own camper. I heard him whistle for Bo, once. Then twice, sharper the second time.

"So, where's Summer now?" Packrat asked, kicking a rock and watching it skitter ahead of us on the dirt road. "I thought she was gonna help today?"

I sighed. "That's why she came this morning. To help. But we had a fight and she went home."

"Home?" Roy chuckled. "What'd ya do?" He nudged my shoulder with his own. Outside the camp office now, he turned to face me. "Beat her in a race? In a bet?"

I shook my head. "She got upset when I told her I'd only counted two kits this morning. She wanted to catch them, raise them. Keep them safe."

Packrat frowned, and pointed a finger at my chest. "Do you believe me now? She and her dad want to get their hands on them. She knows we're watching the den. They can't get close to it. So what better way to get the kits, than for you to hand them over?"

I snorted. "You're nuts!" I shot Roy a can-you-believe-this-guy look.

"No, I'm not!" Packrat insisted. "You just like her so much"—his finger went into my chest—"you can't see the truth!" With each word, he poked me, and with each poke, I backed up a step, until all I saw was red.

I balled up my hands and took a step toward him. "Watch it!" I said.

He did the same until we were nose to nose. "Make me!"

Roy slid between us, putting a hand on each of our chests, his face etched with worry.

"You two are being jerks," he said simply.

I met Packrat's eyes, and even though he still looked mad as a hornet that'd been swatted, he looked kinda sorry, too. I took a step back.

"I just don't get why you don't like her," I said.

My friend ducked his head. He put his hands in his pockets. He started to say more, but his mom came out the office door.

"I thought I heard you three! Come on in, I've got sandwiches for you," she said.

Roy looked at the two of us, a thousand worries all over his face.

Packrat raised his head and, eyes meeting mine, he nodded sadly.

I sighed. I guess we were good again.

Kinda-sorta.

Chapter 22

A fox's narrow snout helps it snoop between rocks and bushes when looking for food.

Before we'd super-cleaned the bathrooms to open them, and before Cat Lady had threatened again to catch the foxes, Mom had asked me one more time if I wanted to go with her and Molly to pick up Dad. He was finally coming home.

"But I want to finish the to-do list," I'd pleaded. "So we look good for *Camping with the Kings*."

And for Dad, I'd added to myself.

She'd leaned out the car window to tousle my hair. Her eyes had dark circles under them, but she looked happier than she had in a long time.

"Cooper, this place isn't going to be as perfect as it normally is in the spring. We just have to accept that. There won't be flowers. The boats won't be at the lake. The docks won't be in the water. And as much as we want it to happen, the campground won't get raked."

"Dad always said leaving the leaves is like leaving paper all over your living-room floor when company comes over."

Mom had smiled at the Dad quote.

"Not exactly, Cooper. It's *leaves*—just nature, doing what nature does. At this point, I'd be happy to just have the water on and tasting chlorine-free, and the bathrooms cleaned. Please, don't worry."

But I did worry. I'd made a promise.

Now, Packrat, Roy, and I stood in the office eating our sandwiches and checking the to-do list. I crossed the opening-the-bathrooms job off. There were way more jobs crossed off than not, thanks to Vern, Packrat's mom, and my friends. That included Summer, whether or not Packrat wanted to admit it.

"Now what?" Roy asked.

I looked at the clock. Three p.m. I wanted so badly to go see the kits, but there were still two jobs written up there that had to be done before the *Camping with the Kings* crew arrived. The first was the raking of the campground—the roads, campsites, playground, and around the buildings. The other was opening all the spigots to let the chlorinated water out of the water lines.

I pointed to the whiteboard. "I want to get them both done," I said.

"I'm in," Packrat said simply. "But how?"

"Walking the campground, opening and closing each spigot one by one to flush the water lines? Dad said it takes four hours by himself. If the four of us do it together—"

"Four?" Packrat raised an eyebrow.

"Four." I didn't leave room to argue. "I bet we'd get it done in an hour and a half, and be able to cross it off the list tonight."

"And do the raking first thing tomorrow morning!" Roy clapped me on the back. "Genius!"

"The raking will be iffy," I warned. "I don't know that we can get it *all* raked and picked up by two when the campers roll in. But if everyone helped"—I gave Packrat a pleading look—"the *four* of us, plus Vern and Mom, too, and maybe Dad driving the dump truck to put the leaves in, we might just make it in time."

Packrat nodded. "Heck, the three . . . I mean *four* of us, could still be raking while our moms checked in campers."

There was my friend!

I called Summer, but she didn't pick up her phone. "She told me her dad had started another project. I bet she can't hear the phone over his music. Want to kayak over and get her?"

"Let me think . . ." Roy put a finger on his chin and stared off into nothingness. Packrat and I laughed, shoving him around a bit, as we grabbed our life jackets and paddles from the store.

I paddled with long, slow strokes, Roy to my right and Packrat on my left. None of us said a word. We just listened to the rippling sounds the water made as the paddles moved through it. The lake was still in the late-afternoon sun, bare trees and white puffy clouds mirrored in its surface. If you looked closely, you could see that the little red buds forming along the branches of the oaks and maples had begun to burst open, showing sprigs of green.

My neighbor Tom raised a hand in greeting as we passed by. In the yard to his right, Boy Scout Brent raised his, too. As Packrat, Roy, and I raised ours in return, I remembered how much the two of them had helped us. Like the time we'd needed round-the-clock eyes on a pair of loons who were building a nest, while a loon-hating camper tried to bully them off the lake.

No one stood in Summer's yard to greet us, but every time I glanced toward her house, I hoped she'd come bursting through the front door to meet us on her beach, like always.

But I could understand if she didn't. I'm not sure I would, after being told to get off her property.

Wooo-OOOOO-oooo-ooo. Funny, how the call of a loon could cause us all to pause in our paddling to look for them. Packrat took a pair of binoculars out of his coat pocket and raised them to his eyes. He grinned and handed them to me, pointing toward the loon raft. One of the loons had its head in the water. When it came up for air, I saw grasses in its beak. It dropped them on the loon raft, poked the nest with its beak a few times, then put its head back in the water for more—a sure sign they'd be nesting again this summer.

Hearing the unmistakable shriek of an eagle, I turned toward the nest, high in a tree to the right of Summer's house. One adult eagle stood on the nest's edge, yelling down at a large, dark bird.

"What's going on?" Packrat asked.

I watched a second adult swoop in to land on the nest and screech along with the first.

"That's a juvenile they're warning off, not an eaglet. Eagles don't get their white heads until they're about five years old, when they're ready to find a mate and lay eggs."

A flash of red on a leg of the juvenile caught my eye, and I tried to get a closer look as it moved back and forth along the branch, hollering up at the adults, who were now flapping their wings, raising their beaks in the air to yell back.

"It's banded!" I cried, when I spied a silver band on the other leg. "Hey! That's last year's chick!"

"No way!" Roy exclaimed.

Packrat shaded his eyes to see better. "So the little guy came back!"

One of the adults gave a shriek and took to the air, wings wide, soaring around the nest. The juvenile looked upward, now silent, as it moved sideways, closer to the trunk of the tree. It reminded me of how I acted when my mom got frustrated and yelled at me.

"And he's still begging for food!" I said.

The adult on the nest started yelling again, just as the eagle in the air swooped down and buzzed the juvenile. It ducked, but held tight to its branch. When buzzed a second time, it hollered once, then got closer to the trunk of the tree. The third time the adult flew close to it, it took to the air. The adult used this chance to chase it, talons forward, screeching. It chased that juvenile, its own child, across the lake and down the other side until it was gone from their territory.

I gave a silent thank-you that my parents weren't like that.

A few paddle strokes later, and we were drifting up onto Summer's beach. I shot a look at her closed front door. Still no sign of her. I tucked my paddle inside the kayak, jumped onto land, and pulled the boat up onto the shore.

Gazing at her house, I took a deep breath and hoped for the gazillionth time that she'd forgive me. I'd only taken a few steps when I realized Roy and Packrat were tagging along.

"Sorry, guys," I said. "I've got to apologize by myself. Then I'll ask her to help us."

Packrat opened his mouth to argue, but Roy clapped him on the back.

"We'll watch from here. It might be fun to see Cooper beg."

When I got to her wooden front door, I knocked once. Loud music seeped from all the windows. A singer called Meat Loaf, I thought. I knocked again, harder this time, then rang the doorbell.

"They wouldn't hear a gaggle of geese fly through the house," I muttered.

Not wanting to go home, now that I'd paddled all the way here, I reached out for the doorknob. When it turned and the door opened, I stepped through.

Whoa.

I was in.

The first thing I noticed was how white and tan everything was. And there was almost no furniture, either.

I'm not sure what I expected, but for the house of an artist, it was kind of, well, blah.

"Hello?" I called. "Hello!"

I shut the door a little louder than I needed to, but still no one came. The music wasn't quite as loud here. Maybe it was being played in a back room.

Follow the music. Find out what her dad really does, whispered the imaginary devil on my left shoulder.

Just find Summer, said the imaginary angel on my right. *Don't go snooping. She won't help you if she catches you in her stuff.*

In front of me, going up the right wall, was a set of stairs to the second floor. To my left was a big dining room with only a long table and four chairs, and nothing else.

I walked straight down the short hall and spied a door on the right, under the staircase.

"Hello?" I called.

I swung the door open to find a fox! Shiny eyes, unblinking, looked up at me. Its golden-red fur, thick and sleek. Poised to run.

I took a quick step backward, and hit a wall.

"Whoa!" I slid sideways and bumped into the open door. "Stay? Good boy—" I stammered, feeling behind me for the way out.

My eyes caught sight of a moose head on the wall, then darted to a snowy white owl perched on a branch on top of a bookshelf. A beaver with a stick between its teeth was on an end table.

A beautiful black-and-white loon, as real as the ones we'd just seen on the lake, rested on a nest made of grasses and lake plants, which in turn sat on a tall, skinny table in the middle of the room.

A turkey, every feather in place, stood on the floor under the window.

Two turtles perched on a log, which looked as if it were rising up out of a puddle of water on a stand.

They all looked so real. As if someone had frozen them in time.

But I knew that wasn't the way it worked.

I was horrified and amazed, all at the same time.

No wonder Summer didn't want us in her house.

She didn't want me to know her father collected dead animals.

Chapter 23

Red foxes have been hunted by humans, for sport and for their fur, since 400 BC.

My eyes went right back to the fox. Even though I now knew it was mounted and stuffed, and it had a big FOR SALE tag hanging off one paw, its eyes still seemed to follow me.

I took one cautious step to peek at that tag. It had $1,000 written on it.

One thousand dollars? For a dead, stuffed, beautiful fox.

That was a lot of money. How much would it be for two adults and five kits?

Summer's voice, explaining what her dad did, rang in my head. *He's an artist. He gets lost in his projects. It's Realism.*

"Cooper?"

I jumped. Summer's eyes were wide as she stepped toward me hesitantly.

"What are you doing here?" Seeing the look on my face, she added, "It's not what it looks like! Honest! Dad, he's—"

I threw out a hand toward the fox.

"It's pretty obvious what he is! No wonder you never let me in here. Not even when it was below zero and we were ice-fishing and I was frozen solid. We always had to go to my house to warm up. Now I get it—how you know so much about foxes. Why the eagles swooping above us for our fish didn't scare you. And how you knew so much about endangered and extinct animals!"

I stormed past her, down the hall to the front door.

"Cooper!" She grabbed my arm, a fistful of shirt, and tried to pull me back. "Please, I'm sorry! Warden Kate was right. I should have told you. I—I can explain!"

I shook off her hand and opened the door, stepping onto her porch.

"I came here because I felt guilty for yelling at you when you wanted to take the kits." I froze. Then I whirled on her, throwing both hands in the air before putting them on the top of my head. "What the heck! I'm such an idiot! I led you right to them!"

I could see Packrat and Roy racing up the hill from the lake.

"I said it before, and I'll say it again: Stay off my land," I told Summer. "Stay away from my campground!"

I jumped down her front steps two at a time, running right past Packrat and Roy.

"What happened?" Roy called to her while walking backwards, trying to keep up with me.

I didn't look back to see her response. And I didn't hear her say anything.

Packrat rushed up beside me. "Cooper? What's going on?"

We'd reached the beach. I was too mad to speak. I pulled my paddle from the kayak and shoved it into the water, resisting the urge to hit something with it. I sensed, rather than saw, Packrat and Roy getting into their own kayaks.

We were halfway across when I realized I hadn't seen her dad.

"We have to go check on the kits. Now."

"But—" started Packrat.

"The water lines—" Roy added.

"Now," I said.

How could I have been so stupid? I kept asking myself over and over. My only excuse was that I had been too busy to notice what she was up to. Packrat had been right all along. Her dad probably wanted to make a little fake fox family. That would be, what—$6,000? Or did kits go for more money? What if they added the mother fox? I picked up my pace, pulled the paddle a little faster and a little deeper.

Summer had been hanging out with me for months. Who knew what else I'd led her to? Shown her? My eagles, loons, wood ducks, the turtle crossing.

When I'd cooled down enough to talk, I explained it all to Roy and Packrat. Roy slapped the water with his paddle.

"All this time, I thought it was Cat Lady trying to get rid of them."

"I'm sorry, Packrat," I said. "I should have listened."

He nodded solemnly. "I wasn't really sure if she was after the kits. It's just that she was acting weird. Going to the trail cam without you. Not around the last couple of days, and now three kits are missing. And she knew stuff! Nature stuff!" In a quieter voice, he added, "To be honest, I was mostly jealous."

Surprised, I stopped paddling to look at him. Roy gave a half laugh. "Even I knew that," he said.

When Packrat looked around me to stare him down, Roy looked up at the sky, then back at me.

"Okay, I was jealous, too," said Roy. "But not as jealous as him!" He tipped his paddle toward Packrat.

"But . . . why?"

"Because she got to hang out on the lake, and the trails, and with *you*, all winter long. And it started to look like she was gonna be hanging out with us all summer long, too." He shrugged. "I wasn't sure I wanted a fourth."

I didn't know what to say. But it didn't matter now anyway.

We locked the kayaks up on my beach, then lugged the life jackets and paddles to my front lawn and dropped them. I'd put them away later. First we had to get to the den. Count the kits.

"On foot?" Roy asked.

"Bikes," I said, jogging toward the shed next to my house, where we'd stored our campground bikes for the winter.

"Now I know you're worried," Roy said. "You never take your bike on the trail."

I had one foot on the pedal, the other ready to push off when I heard my name from the front door of the house.

"Cooper?"

I looked back. Mom stood in the open doorway, a confused look on her face.

"Where are you going? Your dad's home. He wants to see you."

I looked up at the sun and softly groaned to see it touching the treetops. I looked from Packrat's worried face, to Roy's anxious face, to Mom's there-are-no-excuses-you-can-give face.

I dropped the bike and walked slowly into the house.

"We'll stake it out, Cooper. We'll call you!" Packrat shouted as he and Roy started pedaling down the trail.

I walked through the front door, into our living room. Dad lay in his recliner, covered with a blanket and sipping a cup of coffee. He grinned widely when he saw me.

"Cooper! There you are! Mom said you'd gone to visit Summer. I'm glad you had some time off . . ." He stopped, tipped his head to the side, and looked at me. "What's wrong?"

"Nothing."

"You're mad." He took another sip of coffee, giving me a long look over its rim, one eyebrow raised. "At me?"

"What? No!" I moved closer to him. "Why would I be mad at you?"

"Because your mother made you come in for some bonding time instead of letting you check on your fox kits."

"No! Dad. No!" I ran a hand through my hair. "It's complicated."

Dad shifted in his chair and the blanket fell off his arm, the one without the coffee cup. A cast went from his fingers all the way up and over his elbow. I could only stare, as I remembered the whole reason he was sitting there.

Dad raised the arm up, to study it. Then he looked at me with a grin. "Wanna sign it?"

I smiled. "How long do you have to wear it?" I asked.

He turned his arm from side to side.

"I can go back to light duty in three days, buddy. I'm gonna need your help still, but nothing like what you've been doing. It'll be back to school for you after this weekend." He paused to take another sip of coffee, then set the cup down on a coaster on the end table. "You've done a great job, Cooper. Mom says you've had it tough. A lot of water-line leaks."

He frowned. "You know, I'm still confused about that. I mean, I can remember quite clearly blowing all the water out of those lines last fall."

His fingers drummed on the arm of the recliner as he stared out the window. All of a sudden his eyes lit up and he snapped the fingers on his good hand.

"Yes! That's the day I saw the owl, remember? And I called you. You came to check it out."

I did remember! "It was a great horned owl," I said. I pushed the coffee cup aside to sit next to him on the end table. "So if you blew out the water lines, they shouldn't have split?"

"Well, maybe one. Or two at the most. Mom said you had to fix, how many?"

"Five of 'em! And three spigots the day before."

"Doesn't make sense," Dad said. "What did the splits look like?"

"Well, about four inches long."

"Straight or jagged?"

"Straight."

Dad put a hand to his chin. "On the top or underneath the line?"

"On top . . . Oh." It was all making sense. Summer wasn't working with us that day. She could have cut the lines while her dad went to steal the kits.

"Yeah." Dad shook his head. "Someone was messing with you boys. They wanted to keep you busy." He looked at me. "Why?"

I sighed. "That was the day we went from three kits to two."

"Couldn't it just be nature, taking its course?" he asked.

When I shook my head, he asked, "What are you thinking?"

It took a minute for me to be able to speak, because saying the words out loud made it real.

"I think someone is poaching foxes."

"Poaching? For the fur? On our land!" Dad sat straight up. "Have you called the warden?"

"Not yet, but Roy and Packrat are checking right now to see if we're right, and then we're gonna call."

"Good," he said. "That's good."

He yawned loudly. And for the first time I noticed how droopy his eyes were. How purple the other side of his head was.

Dad smiled at me. "Sorry, buddy. You were saying?"

"I think maybe Sum—" My phone buzzed. "It's Packrat."

"Get it," Dad said, leaning back in his recliner. "I want to know what they find."

I stood up and turned away, answering the call. "Yeah."

"Cooper? You aren't gonna like this."

I held my breath.

"There are boot prints all over the bank. Big boot prints. And according to my notes, they match the ones in the store."

"And the kits?"

"One. All we've seen is one."

Chapter 24

*Red fox kits will go out into the world on their own
when they are about seven months old. Males will
travel up to 150 miles to find a new territory.
Females will stay closer to home.*

"One kit?" I gasped.

"What do we do?" Packrat asked over the phone. Before I could
answer, he said, "Uh-oh. My mom's trying to get ahold of me. Roy and I
are heading back. I'll call after I check in."

I turned to find Dad snoring in his chair. Mom came into the room,
smiling at the two of us.

"I was just talking to him and I turned around, and when I turned
back, he was asleep! Just like that!" I snapped my fingers.

Mom pulled the blanket up to Dad's chin. He didn't even stir.

"The doctor said the meds might make him sleepy. And he didn't
get much rest in the hospital. It always feels better to catnap at home."

I nodded. Poor Dad. Once again, I was hit with the guilt of not having had his back. Not protecting him.

Well, I wasn't gonna let that happen with the last kit.

I started to tell Mom about it, but decided she had enough to
worry about. I'd take care of this myself.

I went to my room and called Warden Kate. I got her voice mail,
saying she was away from her phone.

"We're down to one kit," I said, leaving a message. "Can I trap it?
I've got proof someone's poaching them."

Next, I called Packrat and Roy, laying out my plan. Since the warden wasn't around, we had to act fast. We weren't going to let that kit
spend the night alone. Not on my watch.

Cooper and Packrat: Mystery of the Missing Fox

When I was sure Mom was asleep, and when Dad's snores were loud enough to drown out any noise I made, I quietly got out of bed. It felt like I'd been lying there for hours, but when I looked at my watch, it was only ten o'clock. I slid on my warmest sweatshirt and dug out my fingerless gloves, wool socks, and vest. It wasn't cold, but it wasn't summer yet either.

I folded up the blanket from my bed, threw it over my arm, and tiptoed to the door. When I opened it, there sat Molly, cross-legged, wrapped in a blanket.

"What are you doing?" I hissed.

"Waitin' for you." She stood up and I realized she was dressed, ready to go outside, too.

"Oh, no you don't!" I looked down the hall, hoping Mom wouldn't hear us. I turned to Molly, put my hands on her shoulders, and turned her toward her own room.

She shrugged my hands off and turned back to stare up at me.

"Uh-uh. If you don't let me go too, I'll tell."

Time to try something different.

"I'm just going over to Packrat's to sleep."

Molly smiled slowly. "No, you're not. You wanna save the last fox kit. And I wanna come."

"You listened in on my phone call?"

"You talk loud."

Dad's snoring stopped. Molly and I froze, but Molly kept eye contact with me, her baby-blue eyes all lit up with excitement now that she could sense I was waffling. When the snark-snoring started again, I whispered, "Fine! But don't blame me if Mom and Dad find out. You'll be grounded along with me."

"Okay!" she said happily.

"And keep up!"

"I will!"

Halfway to the blind, I wanted to hit my head against a tree. If Mom found out I'd left the house in the middle of the night, I'd be in trouble, big-time. But if she found out I took Molly? Yeah. I might never see the light of day again.

I'd left a note on the kitchen table saying we'd gone to see the foxes. She'd find it when she got up to put on her morning coffee, and think we'd left at the crack of dawn. That might help.

There was a moon, a full moon, and it lit everything up almost like a night-light. We didn't even need a flashlight. Molly stuck close, and she did keep up. Although she had a thousand questions.

"Cooper? What's that sound?"

"Cooper? How do animals see in the dark without flashlights?"

"Cooper? Why do the peep frogs make that noise?"

"Cooper? Who'd want to take a baby fox?"

That last one was the hard one. I didn't want to tell her about Summer just yet. Molly really liked Summer, and I didn't want her to feel like she'd been punched in the stomach, like I did.

When we reached the camouflage tent, Packrat and Roy were inside, playing Go Fish. I held the flap open so Molly could step in.

"Hi, guys!" Her grin practically lit up the tent.

Packrat raised an eyebrow, while Roy fell over laughing. But they both moved over to make room for her.

"What's so funny?" I said, throwing my pillow at Roy.

"Couldn't get out of the house, huh?" He threw my pillow back at me and patted the spot next to him. "C'mon and sit down, Squirt."

"You guys didn't have any trouble getting out?" I asked, as Roy scooped up the cards in the middle of the floor to shuffle them.

"Go Fish?" he asked Molly.

"Yes!"

Packrat picked up the first card Roy dealt him. "We told my mom we were sleeping at your house."

Roy started to lay down my card, but I shook my head.

"I'm going to sit outside. I'll see or hear someone before they get close."

Molly started to yawn, but covered it up with her hand. I threw a pillow her way, smiling when she giggled. "Two games of Go Fish. Then crawl in my sleeping bag, got it?" I unzipped the flap, took one step out. Leaning back in, I said to my friends, "Thanks, guys."

We took turns all night, sitting outside the blind. Everyone but Molly, that is.

At five-thirty the next morning, I'd just switched places with Roy, so he could catch some sleep before we had to start our workday. Other than seeing a skunk waddle by, and smelling it, too, none of us had met with any trouble. Sitting there all alone against a tree trunk, I'd done a lot of thinking. And I realized two things: One, I needed to talk to my dad. Apologize and all. I had to tell him how sorry I was we hadn't gotten the campground perfectly perfect for the *Camping with the Kings* show crew. The three of us and Vern could get the water on this morning before the campers came, but we'd never get the place totally raked now. Not even the playground. I'd failed to keep my promise. But I'd work every day after school next week 'til it was done.

And two, looking back, I wished I'd never gone ice-fishing that first time with Summer. Lying to me about her dad was bad enough, but then she'd gone and almost broken up my friendship with Packrat.

Hearing the tent zipper slowly going down, I turned to see who was up so early. It was that time of day when the night felt like it still wanted to hang out for a little longer, but the sun was pushing against it, forcing it out. I yawned, then almost sucked it back in to see Molly. She looked at me with a silent question. I nodded, and she came to sit next to me, leaning her head on my shoulder. We sat, not speaking, just looking.

The sun rose enough to cast the woods in a golden light. Catching movement at the den, I pointed. Molly got to see the last remaining kit step out into the dawning day.

"Poor little guy," she whispered, as if she were talking to her stuffed elephant. "All alone. His daddy gone and his mommy missing."

When the kit whined, Molly tried singing to him, but he scampered back into his den. I chuckled, but not so she could hear. She had a lot of learning left to do about watching wildlife.

I was beginning to think she and I were going to get into a lot of trouble for nothing, when I heard the unmistakable crunching of shoes on leaves. Then the crack of a stick. A voice.

I threw a couple of pine cones at the tent to wake up Packrat and Roy, and then waited. I couldn't quite see who it was through the trees, but the voice was louder now.

As whoever it was walked through the deep grayness of early dawn, I caught a view of an arm. Then a leg. Then a waist, but not the whole person; I couldn't even see if it was a guy or a girl.

Molly started to rise, trying to figure out where the voice was coming from, too. I tugged her shirtsleeve until she knelt on the ground again, and I put a finger to my lips. The voice was now close enough to hear. I could tell from the tone that the person wasn't happy. But I didn't hear a second voice. Was it someone on the phone?

I heard Roy whisper something, and imagined my two friends peeking out the tent window.

Finally, I could hear the voice say, "I tell you, I didn't hold on to them for too long. They're not dehydrated." It was a guy's voice. "Hiding them wasn't easy. The camp owner, she didn't leave the store much. And those kids are everywhere! I had to make extra work for them, to keep them back at the campground. Then I took those foxes one by one."

A tree trunk hid the face, but I saw a hand thrown out, palm up, as if the speaker were offering up the whole forest.

"I did the best I could, once I found the kits and determined they were the right age."

I balled my hands into fists. Dad didn't goof on the water lines; they'd been cut!

The voice was familiar, but still not quite close enough. In my mind, though, it had to be Summer's dad.

Large black wings swooped low over me, and a big raven landed on the branch above. It walked down, down, down, until it looked me in the eye.

It had a carabiner in its beak.

Bo?

What?

No.

I looked back to the man. But . . . if it was Vern, did that mean he was working with Summer's dad? He *did* know a lot about foxes. Maybe he took them and handed them over to her father. Or did he poach them?

Kill them?

I stared at Bo, wishing I could pick his brain. Get some answers. I held out a hand, and he dropped the carabiner into it. The raven looked at me from one eye, then unfolded his wings and with a hop, took to the air.

Vern stepped into a spot where I could see all of him. His voice was much louder now.

"There's one left. It's been too skittish to come out, but I've got something with me that'll help. The family's too busy getting ready to open today. They won't be anywhere near the den. I'll grab it, collect the others, and bring them to you."

Vern looked up the trail. Toward the water tower. Was that where he had hidden them?

The traitor Vern turned, put a hand on his knee, and rubbed it.

"In town? I'll meet you at the same spot where we sealed the deal." He nodded at whatever the person on the other end of the line was saying. "Sure. Two o'clock. Have the money, or I'll sell the kits to someone else."

Vern stuffed the phone in his pocket and continued toward the den. I scooted over behind the blind, telling Molly with my eyes to stay put. Carefully peeking around the tent, I looked toward the den opening. Even without binoculars, I could see Vern pull something from his coat pocket and sprinkle it on the ground. Food? He then stood to one side of the den and, taking off his coat, he held it out over the opening, waiting for the hungry kit to come out.

Chapter 25

Adult foxes can run up to forty miles per hour over short distances.

I crouched down, low to the ground behind the blind, and looked back at my sister, who was hiding behind a bush. I expected scared or nervous Molly, and was ready to take her straight home, letting Packrat and Roy follow Vern until I could catch up. Instead, my eyes met angry ones.

"He can't take the kit!" she whispered. "What are we gonna do, Cooper?"

I'd never really seen Molly angry. Frustrated, when she couldn't have an ice cream? Sure. A temper tantrum when she was stuck in the store too long? Oh, yeah. But this quiet anger? This was not a Molly I wanted to mess with. But I got it, because I was that angry, too.

I had to know. "What do *you* think we should do?"

"Hit him over the head with something. A big stick, maybe. Then tie him up and call the cops!"

"*Shhhh!*" I warned. "That only happens in the movies, Squirt."

Packrat and Roy had crawled from the blind to join Molly and me behind it. Packrat whispered, "Not who we expected, huh?"

"They could be in on it together."

I glanced around the blind. Vern stood still over the den, waiting for the kit to smell the food and come out. Normally, Vern would be too close. But that kit was probably so hungry, it just might risk it.

Ducking back behind the tent, I whispered, "Okay. We've got to call the warden. But I don't want to take the chance Vern will hear us." I paused, then decided. "I think I know where the other kits are. Let's make sure they're safe. Follow me!"

Roy and Packrat nodded. We hitched our backpacks over our shoulders and, one by one, we crawled in a line through the woods. We were lucky we could take cover in the grayness of dawn. But that wasn't going to last much longer. I took the lead, moving sticks and crunchy leaves out of the way. When I stopped to move a big branch, Molly whispered, "What about George?"

"Who's George?" I asked.

"The last kit! What'll Vern do to him?"

"He wants him alive," Packrat assured her.

"We'll get 'em all back!" Roy promised.

A few yards later, I looked back. Vern was only a speck now, still at the den. The orange early-morning sun was starting to twinkle between the high tree branches. Birds chirped, insects buzzed.

I crouched at Molly's height.

"We've still gotta be really careful not to make noise, 'kay? Watch where you step!"

"Okay."

"Call Warden Kate now," I whispered to Packrat. "Tell her we found the poacher. And I bet I know who the buyer is, too."

Packrat nodded.

We made our way slowly to the trail, where it was easier because the path was already cleared for us. The warden still didn't answer her phone, but Packrat left a message, telling her what we knew.

The farther away we got from Vern, the quicker we moved. Reaching the small hill, we scrambled up. I looked back. Still no sign of him. But we had the advantage. We knew about him, but he didn't know about us.

At the top of the hill, we all stopped to catch our breath.

"Roy, keep a lookout, okay?" I said, handing him my binoculars from my backpack. He got behind the big rock near the duck pond and pulled up his hood to blend in better.

"I'll give the chickadee call if I see him," he said.

I stood with Packrat and Molly, looking over the area. If I was right, and Vern's earlier look toward the water tower meant that he'd taken the kits here, there was only one place to store them. He couldn't climb the tower, and wouldn't dare leave them on top of it anyway. And he wouldn't leave them out in the open, in case of an animal attack.

That left the brick shed. It was locked, but I had my camp keys on me.

"How would Vern get in?" Packrat asked as I slid the key into the lock and turned it.

"Remember when the store got broken into and Dad's keys went missing?" I couldn't believe I'd ever trusted Vern. "He probably watched where Mom put them, when he turned them in for the day. Then he broke in to get them that night, and pretended to find them the next day."

I opened the door. In the minute it took my eyes to adjust to the darkness of the shed, I hoped I was wrong. Wrong about Vern, and Summer's dad, and the foxes.

But I was right.

"Oh! The mother fox!" Molly pointed to a live cage trap, the metal kind that traps the animal inside and won't let it out, but doesn't hurt the animal.

The kits were here, too. Two each, in two plastic cat carriers.

Packrat frowned. "Cat carriers? Cat Lady!"

Molly whispered, "*No!* It can't be! She's so nice."

I glanced at Packrat over Molly's head. Vern *had* been talking to someone on the phone. Was it Summer's dad? Or Cat Lady?

One of the kits whined softly and moved as far back in the carrier as it could go. Molly rushed over, and the mother fox barked. Molly stumbled backward, practically falling on her butt, eyes wide. Packrat shrugged out of his coat and I put it over the mother fox's cage.

Packrat tried calling the warden again. No answer. I heard the beep on the other end of the phone and he whispered into it. "We found them—all of them. At the shed by the water tower."

Packrat put the phone back in his pocket. "Do we take them back to the campground?"

"I'd rather just let them go," I said.

"But Vern will catch them again!" Molly gasped. "These babies can't run fast enough."

I nodded. "And the mother can't carry them all away in time."

"He'll catch us, too, if we go back the way we came," Packrat said. "Only other way is through the bog. The three of us could do it, but with—" He tipped his head down toward Molly.

Nope. A giant dark pool of stagnant water, made from melting snow and spring rains, stretched for yards and yards in that direction. No way Molly would get through it.

Roy gave a chickadee call. I jogged over, crouching down beside him. He held out the binoculars. It was hard to see Vern through the trees, but he was coming. And it looked like he was carrying a burlap bag.

The last kit?

"We don't have much time," Roy warned.

I looked around. We couldn't make a run for it through the bog with Molly. Back down the path wasn't an option; Vern would find us. But we couldn't leave the foxes behind either!

I looked up. The tower. We'd hidden up there once before, from Cat Lady. She'd passed right by, not even knowing we were there. Could we fool Vern, too?

Roy saw my gaze. "Vern can't climb with that knee."

I nodded. "I'm sure the warden will be here soon." At least, I hoped she would be. I put a hand on Roy's shoulder. "Stay here. Call again when he's halfway."

Packrat and Molly had brought out the cat carriers. They weren't big, but climbing with them wasn't going to work.

I sighed. "I think we have to let the mother fox go," I said quietly.

"No!" Molly cried. "What about her babies?"

"Those we can handle with gloves. But the mom isn't going to let us handle her without a fight, and we can't climb with the trap cage. I don't want to risk dropping the mom."

Packrat was already pulling out gloves. He and I looked for handles on the live-trap cage to carry it. There was one on Packrat's side, but I couldn't find the one on mine. Wait! That's because it was in my pocket!

"The handle we found on the bush. It's from this trap!" I said, tying a piece of rope to my side of the cage to create a new handle. "That time the fox was shrieking? In the middle of the night? She was being trapped and taken from her kits."

Packrat and I lifted the coat-covered cage to carry it to the edge of the clearing, closest to the bog. Setting it down with the opening facing the tree line, I had Molly and Packrat stand behind me.

I folded back the coat. Turning to Molly, I put a finger to my lips. "I saw the warden do this once. Be very quiet. We just let her go. We'll get the kits to her later, after the bad guys are caught."

Molly nodded. Her eyes were shining with excitement.

I held up three fingers, then two, then one, and I opened the door.

At first, nothing happened. I tapped the back of the cage, gently. She barked.

I cringed. If Vern heard that, he'd be here double time.

"C'mon, c'mon," I urged. "No one's gonna hurt you."

"Run!" Molly whispered. "We'll get your babies to you, I promise!"

I'm sure the fox didn't understand her, but it did poke its head out of the cage, then took off like a shot into the bog.

We watched for half a second. Because that was all we had.

Chapter 26

*Foxes use their thick, furry tails for balance, as a
warm cover when it's cold, and as a signal flag to
communicate with other foxes.*

I picked up Packrat's coat and handed it to him before grabbing the
now-empty fox cage. We threw it in the shed, dropping it on the floor.
Next, I slowly opened one of the cat carriers. The kits backed up inside,
as far as they could go.

"It's okay, little guys!" I slowly put my gloved hand in, knowing
the kits must be terrified to see this ginormous brown thing coming at
them. I picked one up by the scruff of the neck, just like its mom would
do. It went limp. Packrat opened my backpack, dumped the contents on
the floor of the shed, and opened it as wide as it could go. I put that kit
inside, added the second one, and we pulled the zippers almost shut,
leaving room for air to get in. Then we did the same thing with the second carrier, putting those kits in Roy's now-empty backpack.

"Not your coat?" Molly asked.

Packrat shook his head, saying, "They have more room in the
backpack."

Roy gave the chickadee call. I stood and shaded my eyes. Roy was
jogging over.

Vern was almost here.

"Go," I said, handing Packrat my backpack of kits.

"But—" He looked at Molly.

Roy arrived. "Take these kits," he said. "Cooper and I have the Squirt."

Packrat nodded. He ran to the tower and, using the Xs in the
water-tower legs, started to climb.

Roy got down to Molly's level. "I'll be right behind you, okay? Just
climb up. Don't look down. Packrat will take your hand at the top."

"Aren't you coming?" Molly asked, glancing at me as we race-walked to the tower. For the first time since this whole thing started, she looked scared.

"I'm right behind you and Roy," I said. "You can do this. Step on."

She took the first couple of steps slowly, then quickly climbed the rest of the way like a monkey. When she reached Packrat, he put out a hand to help her onto the catwalk.

I looked back to the shed. We'd left the door open and the carriers lying about as if we'd come and gone already. I put the second backpack on, feeling the kits moving around a bit as I put a foot into the first X and began to climb. Above me, Packrat was climbing the ladder from the catwalk to the roof. Molly was making her way along the catwalk, her back against the water tank, Roy holding her hand. I reached up and pulled myself onto the metal grates of the walkway. Molly looked around Roy to me.

I waved her on with my hands, not wanting to speak, scared Vern would hear.

She turned to climb the ladder, Roy only one rung behind, his body shielding her, in case she slipped. Packrat leaned over from where he was lying on the roof, reaching down to help her over the top. She was quick, and scurried onto the roof, no problem.

Suddenly, trees got blurry, and the sky tilted. My world shifted!

I threw all my weight toward the water-tank wall, stomach first so I didn't squish the kits. With my feet as close to the tank as possible, I took deep breaths, willing the rolling and rocking to stop. I heard Molly gasp, and Roy tell her to sit down.

"You okay?" Roy whispered down.

I slowly opened my eyes. Everything was back to where it should be. What had happened? I lifted a foot to take a step and Roy whisper-called, "Careful! The catwalk looks loose or something."

Cooper and Packrat: Mystery of the Missing Fox

A chickadee call sounded from the roof—Packrat signaling that Vern was closing in.

I shuffle-stepped my way along the catwalk to the ladder, practically hugging the wall. When I reached the ladder and swung one foot onto the lowest rung, I let all the air out of my lungs. I'd made it! Looking down at the catwalk, I saw the problem: That one section of grate I'd been standing on had pulled free. The support bar underneath looked like it was attached to the tower, but it really wasn't.

I'd gotten lucky.

Gonna have to tell Dad about that, I thought, as I climbed the rungs.

Hearing a noise above me, I looked up. Three sets of eyes stared down. Molly shot me a big smile, but then her eyes got wide. Roy's hand grabbed her shirt and all three of their faces disappeared.

"Cooper?" Vern asked from the ground. "Shouldn't you be helping your dad open the campground?"

Chapter 27

*A fox might steal a chicken if it's desperate, but these
omnivores actually prefer smaller prey like squirrels,
rabbits, mice, and even caterpillars and beetles.*

I looked down at Vern from halfway up the ladder, the kits moving
slightly in my backpack. Above me, Roy whispered, "Darn it!"

Vern took a couple of rolling steps forward, one hand gripping the
opening of a burlap bag , a rope tied loosely around the top. He shielded
his eyes with the other as he asked again, "Shouldn't you be helping your
dad?" His mouth turned upward like a smile, but the rest of his face didn't
look happy to see me. Especially his narrowed, sharp eyes.

"I came to check"—I looked around for something, anything, and,
seeing the tip of the water-tower roof, and the wire running from it—
"the valve. For the level of the water. First job today. Open all the faucets
and"—I took one hand off the ladder to wave it over the trees and bog
and campground—"release the water in all the water lines to get the
chlorine out. That can, you know, cause a lot of stress on the well and . . ."

I trailed off. I knew I was babbling, but I really had no idea what to
do now. Except fake it and stall for time.

Vern walked closer, still shading his eyes. The bag he carried in
his other hand wiggled a little. Anger surged in me, as hot as a roaring
campfire.

"Hey," the taunting words popping from my mouth before I could
take them back, "whatcha got there?"

And as I looked down at him, and Vern looked up at me, I knew
that he knew that I knew exactly what was in the bag.

Me and my big mouth.

He gave me one more leveled stare, then turned and limp-walked
toward the shed. Seeing all the crates and the trap empty, he swore.

I started climbing up the ladder again, fast.

"What'd you do with them, kid?"

I looked over my shoulder to find Vern holding the live-trap cage in both hands, the burlap bag now on the ground. He glared at me. I stared back. Finally, he tossed the trap aside and limp-jogged back toward the tower. Pointing a finger up at me, he yelled, "I want those kits, and I want them now! I'll wait all day if I have to."

"He doesn't have them!" a familiar voice called out. Summer came rushing up the hill, green eyes blazing.

"What are *you* doing here?" I yelled. "Did your dad get tired of waiting for Vern to bring back the foxes?"

She looked up at me, eyes flashing. "Smart! You figured it all out."

Vern looked between us. "What the heck are you talking about? Her dad ain't getting them!"

Summer crossed her arms. "As a matter of fact, *I* have them. And you're gonna have to pay me if you want them."

I could've sworn I heard Roy whisper, "I'm so confused."

Packrat shushed him.

Vern turned on Summer. "*You* have them?"

"Me!" Summer stood tall. "What are they worth to you? I know what they're worth to me. Did you know people will pay a thousand dollars for a stuffed fox? What do you think they'll offer for a whole family in front of a fake den? All seven of them—"

Vern grabbed a fistful of her shirt, pulling her in until his face was right next to hers. "Seven?" he barked.

Summer lifted her chin, her eyes sliding to mine. "Warden Kate *gave* my dad the dead male in the trap."

"I don't want to kill them." He shoved her back. "They're worth more to me alive! You're gonna show me where they are!"

"I am not!"

Vern half pulled, half pushed her toward the trail as Bo soared over them, calling down.

"No!" I called from the ladder, watching Summer struggling in his grip. "What are you doing? Leave her alone!" I shouted up to Roy and Packrat. "Call home!"

Packrat leaned over to whisper, "I left my phone in the shed after I called Warden Kate! And we emptied your backpack there, too."

I had to tell Vern we had the foxes. Who knew what he'd do to Summer! I opened my mouth, but a small sound had me closing it again. Vern must have heard it too, because he froze. Summer kept struggling, trying to break his grip on her arm, but hearing another cry, she, too, went still.

It was strange. A small animal-like whine. Summer looked up at me, eyes wide. I shook my head at her. It hadn't come from my backpack.

Bo landed on the ground, beside the shed. He paced back and forth. *Cruuuuuck! Cruuuuuck!*

The whine answered.

"Over here!" Vern pulled Summer toward the side of the shed.

Packrat and Roy leaned over the edge of the tower roof.

"What was that?" Roy whispered.

"Did we forget one?" Packrat wondered.

Vern let go of Summer, and she dropped to her knees.

"You lied! They're under here!" he cried. Down on all fours now, he put his hand in the hole under the shed, elbow-deep. Feeling around, he grinned, then gave a whooping laugh as he pulled his arm out.

But what he held wasn't brownish red. It was black and white.

"A skunk?" Roy cried, laughter in his voice.

"No—" Packrat began.

"Fred!" Summer cried.

Seeing the cat must have been the last straw, because Vern stood up, held out the hissing, struggling cat in one hand, and drew back his foot, gearing up to kick it.

Summer rushed him, hands out, and pushed him, hard. Bo flew around Vern's head, cawing loudly, talons down.

I heard a loud, angry cry. "Leave Fred alone, you big bully!"

But that hadn't come from Summer. It came from above me. Molly! She stood on the water tower roof, fists clenched.

"Get down!" I hissed.

But I was too late. Vern had seen her. He looked from Summer, to me, to Molly, and in seconds, he'd sized up the entire situation. All four of Fred's paws were moving, claws out, until they made contact with Vern's arm, and he dropped the cat. Fred ran from the commotion, ducking back under the shed.

Vern grabbed Summer's arm again. "Ow!" she cried.

He dragged her to the shed, threw her inside, tossed the burlap bag after her, closed the door, and locked it. I winced, as much from the kit hitting the ground like that as from watching Summer pound on the door, racing from window to window, eyes wide.

In the quiet that followed, a bark came from the bog.

And an answering whine came from my backpack.

Ever so slowly, Vern looked my way. I climbed the last two rungs on the ladder, wanting to put as much distance between Vern and me as I could. Reaching the top of the water tower, I stood and looked down at him. No words were spoken, by any of us. The raven flew to the catwalk, halfway, as if it didn't know which side to take.

Finally, Vern spoke.

"I'll be taking those kits now. You have nowhere to go."

Chapter 28

An adult red fox has forty-two teeth.

Vern had only taken two steps toward the ladder when Molly yelled, "Don't you touch these baby foxes or my brother will hurt you!"

Hurt *him*? I rolled my eyes. She didn't realize what I'd done. Instead of bringing us to a safe hiding place, I'd led us here. Now we were cornered. The only way down was the way we'd come, and Vern was there, waiting.

Summer started pounding on the shed door again, hollering, "Help! Help!" Her voice was faint from behind the brick walls.

Vern turned to yell at her. "Shut up! Nobody will hear you calling from there!"

Packrat's face lit up. The minute Vern turned his back to us, my friend stared in Summer's direction, while putting his right hand to his ear, with the thumb and pinky finger stretched out, and the other three curled in. He pointed to it over and over with his left hand.

Roy scoffed, nodding toward the shed. "You want her to call you when this is all over?" He put a hand on Packrat's shoulder. "Dude, I don't think this is the time—"

Packrat's ears turned red.

"No! I get it!" I said, copying Packrat as I whisper-explained to Roy. "My phone! It's on the floor of the shed."

Summer had stopped banging on the door to look out the window. We knew the minute she saw us. She tipped her head to one side in an I-don't-get-it kind of way, then disappeared from sight. Vern must have seen her move, because he turned around to look up at us. I scratched my head and looked up at the clouds, while Packrat coughed in his hand. Roy shouted down, "What are *you* looking at?"

Vern approached one of the tower legs, looking for an easy way up.

Summer reappeared in the window of the shed, and when she was sure Vern wasn't looking her way, she gave us a thumbs-up, the phone in her hand.

"It's a standoff until the warden gets here," Roy assured me. "Vern can't climb with that bum leg."

Vern put his foot on the first X.

"Darn it!" said Roy.

I realized I'd more than messed up. I'd messed up in the extreme. Molly, the fox kits, and two of my friends were stuck on this water tower. Summer was locked in the shed. We were all cornered by the bad guy, just like in a movie. It was too far to jump. We couldn't even lower the foxes down!

"We've got to stall him for as long as we can! So the warden or Mom and Dad can get here," I whispered. "Packrat, whatcha got in your coat?"

He emptied one pocket after another, dropping stuff on the roof at our feet. Binoculars, a bungee cord, some pieces of rope, the double-baggie with the T-shirt and sneakers, the two carabiners from Bo, one steel water clamp, a Super Soaker, a flashlight—wait!

I pointed to the yellow-and-red Super Soaker and gave Packrat a what-the-heck look.

He gave me a sheepish smile. "I was gonna pay Summer back the next time I saw her. You know, for dumping the glass of water over my head."

Vern swore from somewhere below us. I rushed to the edge to find him still on the leg of the tower, struggling to raise his bum knee high enough to make the climb. It was slow going, but he was doing it.

"Molly, sit with the kits and make sure they don't get brave and wiggle out of the backpacks," I said. She nodded and moved with the backpacks to the center of the tower, by the lightning rod.

Bo flew in and landed next to her. *Cruuuuuck! Cruuuuuck!* He walked over to one of the backpacks, pecking at a side pocket.

"No! No helping that bad man!" Molly said, giving him a gentle nudge.

I slid the Super Soaker over to Roy.

"Fill it at the hatch, okay? It's all we've got to keep him from climbing that second ladder."

"It's not all we've got," Packrat said with a grin.

We watched him go to the side of the tower and lean over to put his hand on the overflow pipe. The opening where water flowed from was positioned right next to the ladder. Packrat knelt down and grabbed the rope that would open it and send water gushing to the ground below.

I slapped him on the back. "Perfect!"

Roy ran to the hatch, opened it, and dipped the Super Soaker in the water to fill it. "This is going to be awesome!" he said.

I lay down on the tower's roof and leaned over the edge. Vern had finally gotten to where he could put his hands on the catwalk. He looked up, eyes on me like a coyote on a rat. Quicker than I thought, he pulled himself up.

Roy rushed back to lie next to me. Packrat nodded my way from his post. "Say when."

I wasn't sure which I wanted more now—for my parents to get here, or for this fox poacher to come a little closer so we could start the water fight.

Vern put a hand on the water tank and slowly limp-walked along the catwalk. His chest rising and falling from the climb, he stopped to lean over and look down the tower leg he'd just climbed.

Suddenly, a sharp metal-on-metal scraping sound filled the air, hurting my ears. Vern's body swayed toward the tank, then away, then back to it.

The loose panel on the catwalk!

Vern fell to his knees, the section of catwalk floor hanging at an odd angle. He slowly, slowly crawled, until he got his hands on the next section and carefully pulled himself onto it. When he was safely sitting, he yelled up at me between heavy breaths. "You'll be the first one I toss off the top into the duck pond!"

"I don't think so!" I called down.

Packrat's eyes were on me, begging me to give the word. Vern was sitting right underneath the overflow valve.

I shook my head. Vern was cursing, yelling threats. Finally, he stood and looked up at us.

"Now!" I called.

Packrat pulled the rope. Water poured from the pipe, gallons a minute, right onto Vern's head. He swayed a little, right, then left, then right, before swinging himself around, arms open wide, to fall against the tank, hugging it like it was his only lifeline. Which it was.

Packrat closed the pipe. Vern tried to yell at us, but sputtered instead, spitting water everywhere. He slid over, out from under the downspout, and ran a hand over his face.

Roy took aim with the Super Soaker. "My turn?" he pleaded.

"Go for it!" I said. "Make him back up. Don't let him climb that ladder."

I didn't have to tell Roy twice. He hit Vern right on the top of the head.

Vern looked up, eyes shooting daggers.

Roy soaked him in the face.

Vern growled. Packrat called down, "Oh, Vern!" His hand opened and closed around the rope on the drainpipe.

"You wouldn't dare!" Vern cried.

Roy, Packrat, and I laughed out loud. If Vern knew us better, he'd know those were fighting words!

Packrat pulled down a little. The water sprinkled.

"You little—"

Then Packrat turned the pipe, positioning it right over Vern's head again. Grinning widely, he opened the pipe full force, which had Vern tank-hugging again.

He raised a fist halfway, and yelled something that sounded like *Spew spittle spats*! But we knew what he was saying.

I caught sight of Summer in the shed window, jumping up and down in excitement. I gave her a thumbs-up.

Roy ran back to refill the Super Soaker. I signaled Packrat to keep the water coming. It was pretty obvious Vern didn't dare move while the water was on. It made the catwalk too slippery.

Above all the commotion, I heard Molly say, "No! Bad bird!"

Looking over to where she sat, I saw Bo with a silver carabiner in his beak.

"It's okay, Molly. Just watch those kits!"

"Cooper!" Packrat called.

Roy rushed back with the Super Soaker and dropped to the roof to aim.

Packrat whispered, "The water level of the tank is below the overflow. I'm out. No more ammunition."

Every time Vern looked up at us, Packrat gripped the rope and stared down, daring him to make a move for the ladder. Eventually Vern would figure it out, I knew. We weren't going to be able to hold him there much longer.

"Let me at him!" Roy growled.

"Wait for his move," I advised. "Once you're out of water, he'll be up here faster than you can fill it again."

I looked at the heap of stuff from Packrat's coat. We could throw it all down, one at a time, onto Vern's head. But it'd only slow him down, not stop him.

HAH HAH, HAH, Hah!

Bo was laughing at us? The raven paced on the wire that ran from the lightning rod, over the duck pond, and down to the shed roof.

"This isn't playtime!" I scolded. "Shoo!"

HAH HAH, HAH, Hah!

Bo took flight, soaring around the tank over our heads before flying down to land next to the shed.

If only we could fly off this tower, too.

"Zip line!" I heard Roy whisper from behind me.

I shook my head. My friend was crazy. Unless . . .

I looked at the old power line, running from the thick metal lightning rod down to the shed roof.

"Zip line!" Packrat said, eyes twinkling.

I grinned. Zip line.

"What's a zip line?" Molly asked.

Uh-oh. My grin faded. I'd forgotten about Molly.

"I'll piggyback her," Packrat offered. "I do it all the time. She puts her feet in my pockets for balance."

"What about rappelling down the back of the tower before Vern gets up?" I offered, looking for a different way out.

Packrat shook his head. "I only have a couple of short pieces of rope."

Roy pressed the trigger of the Super Soaker, eyes on Vern. "Those ropes could be handles. Put them through the carabiners Bo gave you."

"There's only two—"

"I have one!" I said. "Bo just gave it to me by the den!" I dug deep in my pocket and pulled it out.

Roy gave another quick squeeze of his trigger. Vern cursed below.

"Take the soaker, Packrat," Roy said. "I'll make something."

When Packrat took Roy's position at the Super Soaker, I heard Vern laugh.

"Don't have any more water, do you?" Vern's voice came from the catwalk. "Brats!"

Packrat pulled the Super Soaker trigger. "No, but I've still got this!"

Over his shoulder, he whispered to Roy, "Go. I'll distract him with this when you take off."

Roy slid a length of rope through the carabiner and tied the ends together in a figure-eight knot. "One of the strongest, when it comes to holding weight," he explained. "I'll go first, test out the line." He quickly made up two more zip-line gadgets.

Roy clipped the carabiner to the wire, moved it back and forth a bit to make sure it would slide, then grabbed hold of the rope. "Here goes nothing!"

"Wait!" I brought him one of the kit-filled backpacks, and helped him put it on. Handing him my camp keys, I said, "Get Summer out of the shed."

He gave me a tense nod, then took a running start, lifted his knees, and dropped off the side of the roof.

I ran over to watch. He didn't fly liked I'd hoped, but he did sail quietly over the duck pond, dropping to the ground in a crouch, then running to hide behind the shed. He peeked around the corner and flashed us a thumbs-up. Slowly, he inched his way to the door, my keys in his hand.

I looked at Vern, who only had eyes for Packrat and his giant squirt gun.

Roy let Summer out.

I knelt by Molly. "I'm sending you with Packrat, okay?"

She nodded.

"You're going piggyback. Don't make a sound, so Vern doesn't see."

Molly hugged me tight. "You'll be right down?"

"I will. With the rest of the kits."

I raced over to Packrat, who had a worried look on his face.

"Go," I said, taking the Super Soaker and giving Vern a quick shot of water to make him stay put next to the ladder. Ignoring the poacher's swearing, I nodded toward the line. "Don't wait for me. Run for home."

Packrat looked like he was going to say something, but I butted in.

"I got us into this. I have to get us out."

Packrat nodded. "I'll do it for Molly."

I gave Vern another shot of water. "Stay there!" I yelled, "and I won't shoot again."

I glanced over my shoulder. Packrat stood with Molly's arms clutched around his neck, her feet in his pockets. He said something to her and she gave a little smile. The second he leapt, I shot Vern with water again.

He shook his fist at me. "That's it!"

And he started to climb. I gave him a shot of water. Then another. He just ducked his head into it and kept coming. I watched Roy dash out from behind the shed to grab Packrat by the feet and stop him, so he and Molly would land safely on the ground.

I pulled my water-gun trigger. Nothing. I tried again. Not even a drop.

Vern looked at me, a slow smile curling upward. I dropped the soaker on his head, which surprised him so much he stumbled and slipped down a couple of rungs on the ladder.

I scrambled back, still on all fours, and turned to race to the zip line. My right hand slipped on the double-buggie and my wrist twisted. I fell on my stomach, hitting my chin on the roof.

A hand wrapped around my ankle.

"You ain't going nowhere!" Vern yelled.

He was leaning up and over the roof edge, his feet still on the ladder rungs, eyes nothing but slits.

"They won't leave," he said, tipping his head toward the ground, where Summer, Roy, and Packrat stood looking up. Molly had her hands in front of her eyes, her fingers spread so she could peek. "Not while I have you, anyway."

He looked down at them.

"Drop the kits!" he hollered. "Back away, or I pull him over the edge."

Something warm and soft dropped on my hand. Glancing down, I saw blood. I swiped at my chin with the back of my other hand and felt the sting as my skin met the gash there.

Looking around frantically for something to help me, I saw movement on the roof. The backpack! The kits were wiggling inside it! And it was skittering down the slight incline of the roof.

"The kits!" I cried. "They're gonna fall!"

Chapter 29

*Fox hunting with dogs was a popular sport in the
United States during the late 1920s and early 1930s;
almost five thousand foxes were captured each year in
Maine alone during that time.*

"Nice try, kid! I ain't letting go!" Vern yelled, as I watched the kits'
backpack head for the edge of the tower roof.

I struggled, but Vern's grasp became tighter on my ankle. My
hands searched for something, anything. I threw the flashlight over my
shoulder, but it missed Vern by a mile. With the backpack just inches
from falling, Packrat, Roy, and Summer rushed to get underneath it. I
tossed the bungee cord at Vern, and he caught it in his free hand. Tucking
it in his pants pocket, he laughed. "I'll use it to tie you up!"

I scrambled for a handhold, another weapon, anything! What I
found was the double-baggie.

Yes!

I looked for the backpack, and gasped. It was on the edge, teetering
back and forth as the kits moved around inside.

"No!" I cried, kicking and straining to break free as the backpack
slowly rolled off the roof edge.

I closed my eyes, imagining the poor kits landing in a heap—

And I heard cheering from below. *Cheering?* And Packrat calling,
"Cooper! Quick!"

I opened my eyes. The backpack strap had gotten hung up on a
bent sheet of roof metal!

I ripped open the double-baggie, gasping in and holding a clean
breath of air. I threw one stinky sneaker over my shoulder. Vern ducked.
I threw the second. He just tugged me closer, pulling on my leg for
leverage to help him up the last couple of rungs on the ladder.

"You kids, always in the way." Vern growled the words, as I unfolded the T-shirt. "Should've listened when I told you to stay away from those foxes!" He stopped, sniffed the air. "What's that god-awful smell?"

In one motion, I rolled onto my back and stretched the cat-pee T-shirt out in both my hands. Just as I met Vern's eyes, I tossed the T-shirt over the poacher's head. One giant yank, then a kick of my free foot, and he let my other foot go. My friends' voices rose in a cheer.

I scrambled over to the backpack, gently pulling it from the slats, up onto the roof. I felt the little guys wiggling, but couldn't take the time to open it and check on them. I put my arms through the straps, snapped the last carabiner on the line, and took two giant steps, the rope handle tight in my hands. Right before I leapt, I felt hands grab for my sweatshirt.

But Vern was too late.

I zipped over the duck pond, the wind making my eyes water as I swung back and forth on the line. Packrat and Roy grabbed hold of my shirt and feet, stopping me at the end of the line.

That was so cool!

Molly hugged my waist while Packrat and Roy gave me high fives. Hearing cursing and yelling, we looked up to find Vern tossing the bungee cord I'd thrown at him earlier over the old power line.

Summer grabbed my arm. "He's coming down!"

I knew he would. I looked around for something, anything that would help us once he was on the ground. Even the frogs and the birds and the insects had gone silent.

Vern stepped backward, pausing long enough to shoot us an I'm-coming-for-you look. He took two big steps, then leapt forward from the tower. He slid down, down, down, but then he slowed. And slowed some more, until he'd stopped a little more than halfway down. The line sagged. He swayed from side to side, feet moving like he was treading water. The line sagged some more.

Crack! Vern dropped a couple of feet, then bounced up and down.

I held my breath. Molly covered her eyes. "I can't look!"

Crack! The line broke off the shed roof. Vern screamed as he fell straight down, arms and legs frantically moving until, *splash!* He landed right in the duck pond, just missing Oscar's giant rock.

We all stared. Should I rush in? Pull him out? Leave him there?

The minute Vern came up, sputtering, I yelled, "Run!"

We could be faster than him, I knew. Maybe I could still fix this. I could get the kits safely home to their mother. Molly, home to Mom and Dad.

"Go!" I shouted.

"Stop! I need those kits!" Vern took three shuffling steps in the waist-deep water, then fell again. "You ruined everything!" He slapped the water, splashing himself in the face. "They were going to pay for my surgery!"

I yelled back, pointing my finger at him.

"I knew it! You wanted their pelts! It's illegal to hunt foxes on private property! And it's illegal to hunt them *anywhere* in April!"

"Not their pelts," he snarled. He stood, bracing his twisted arm with his good hand and wincing in pain. "I wanted to sell them. Give them good homes."

Good homes? What the heck was he talking about?

Seeing me hesitate, his eyes turned pleading. "I can get eight hundred dollars apiece for them as pets. I'll give you a cut of that."

"I don't want your money! They need to be with their mother. You took their father from them!"

"That was a mistake. I didn't expect the coyote to go after it."

I heard, rather than saw, the gang coming back slowly. I never took my eyes off Vern as he spoke.

"I only catch them, give them to people who train them," Vern said. "Then *they* give them to good homes. Like a dog or a cat. Think about it, Cooper." Now knee-deep in the pond, he held out a hand, like he was offering me a prize. "It'd give your kits a much better chance of survival than if you let them go. They'd have a much longer life. They wouldn't have to worry about harsh winters. Cars on roads. Coyotes. Trappers."

I wavered. I could almost see his point.

"What if the female doesn't take them back?" Vern warned. "What if she thinks they aren't good enough to raise anymore?"

"What parent would think such a thing?" My father's voice boomed from behind me.

"Daddy!" Molly called.

I turned to see him coming up the bank, Warden Kate right behind him.

Molly raced forward to hug him.

When he reached me, he wrapped his good arm around my shoulder. "You okay?" he asked, as he squeezed me into his side.

I nodded.

Warden Kate moved around Dad.

"Where's the poacher?" she asked. Seeing Vern standing in the pond, wet and broken, she said, "Never mind."

Vern stumbled through the muck of the duck pond, water dripping from his hair. He fell again, face-first. When he came back up, he had some kind of plant hanging off one ear like an earring. He kept swatting at it, but it wouldn't budge. In the pond, a frog croaked in annoyance.

"A toad in a frog pond," Packrat said, which had us all cracking up.

"Wait!" I cried, walking toward the pond.

Vern looked up at me and smiled. He held out a hand.

"I knew you'd change your mind," he said. "You're a smart kid."

I marched into the water, right past him, to the giant rock. Sitting on top was my three-legged frog, Oscar.

"Where have you been?" I asked, holding him in one hand and stroking the patch of skin between his eyes with the other. I stepped

out of the pond, and Warden Kate stepped in to help Vern out. She called for backup on her radio and then started firing questions at Vern.

Looking up from inspecting Oscar, I saw that Mom had joined Dad. I sighed. We were all in trouble now. But I didn't care. The kits were safe—

The kits!

I quickly handed Oscar to Mom, then took off my backpack to set it gently on the ground. Roy did the same with his backpack, and Summer with the burlap bag. Packrat dug deep into his pockets to give us all our gloves.

Slowly, we opened the bags, one by one, rolling down the sides. The kits blinked in the bright sunshine, none of them looking hurt. Just a little scared.

"We have to let them go, don't we?" Summer asked quietly.

I smiled at her.

"I want to hold one!" Molly said, kneeling down. I opened my mouth, but she said, "I mean, I *wish* I could. I know I can't."

The kits looked around, but didn't try to get out of the bags.

Warden Kate came over, Vern in handcuffs behind her. "Where's the mother?" she asked.

"We let her go before we climbed the tower," I said.

"Climbed the tower?" Mom exclaimed.

"Yeah!" Molly's face lit up. She jumped up, her hands waving a mile a minute toward the tower and the shed. "And we were gonna hide, but then Summer got locked in the shed by Vern, and he got really mad when he found out we had the kits, so he climbed up to throw us off, and Roy shot him—"

"Shot him!" Dad's eyebrows went right up into his hairline.

"With water," Packrat explained.

Molly didn't stop. "And then we zipped down the line."

I sighed. "Zip-lined."

Mom opened her mouth and closed it several times.

"That's what I said! And Cooper fought with Vern, and he threw a T-shirt on him, and then he saved the bag of kits when it almost rolled off the edge, but it got caught on the roof!" Molly beamed up at everyone in turn. No one spoke for a minute, until Warden Kate cleared her throat.

"Well. Then."

A sharp, short bark came from just beyond the tree line. The kits looked toward it and whined. The biggest and bravest took a few steps that way, wagging its tail. I squinted, and it took a minute, but I found the red face of the mother fox in the shadows of the trees.

Cooper and Packrat: Mystery of the Missing Fox

The warden put her gloves on. She picked up each kit by the scruff of the neck.

"Just like its mom does," she explained. "Their bellies seem to be half full. They're hydrated. I don't see any reason why we can't let them go back to their mom." She looked at all five of us. "Five kits for five kids." Then she smiled.

Vern looked like he was going to cry.

Each one of us picked up a kit by the scruff of the neck, just as the warden showed us. Then we cupped their bottoms in our other hands, in case they tried to wiggle free. We crouched down to make ourselves smaller, and moved nearer to the tree line, closer to where I'd seen the mom. She ran back into the woods, but not very far.

I put mine down first, pushing it gently on its butt, toward the trees.

"Go on," I said, as my friends set their kits down too. We all backed up.

The mom barked. Two of the kits quickly scamper-waddled toward her, as the five of us backed up slowly, staying low to the ground, never taking our eyes off the kits. The third and fourth kits followed. One more sharp bark from the mom had the fifth one slowly trotting toward her, too.

"I can't wait to see the kits tomorrow!" Molly clapped her hands together. I put my hand on her shoulder and shook my head, as the last kit disappeared into the brush. "She'll move them somewhere safer. Vern, and we, messed with the den one too many times."

As we all stood up, Warden Kate explained.

"After Vern trapped the male fox and it was attacked, he live-trapped the mom to get her out of the way. I believe him when he says it was never his intention to kill the foxes. With the vixen out of the way, the kits would get hungry. That allowed him to lure them from the den with food, then trap them. But Vern swears he didn't leave the T-shirt and sneakers outside the den. Someone else is responsible for that."

"This morning, we heard Vern talking on the phone with someone, about meeting in town!" I said. "And that they'd better have the money!"

"Yeah!" Packrat said. "I bet that's who put the stuff by the den! The buyer!"

"They were going to meet at two o'clock," Roy said.

The warden wrote it all down in her notebook. "I'll get his phone and see if I can track the number."

"C'mon," Dad said. "Let's go home. We've already had way more excitement than we should for one day, and we still have a campground to open."

Warden Kate waved us along. "I can finish up here. I'll be down later to get all your statements."

Bo flew in, landing by the corner of the shed. In all the excitement, I'd forgotten all about him! Where had he gone?

Was that something in his mouth? He hopped around the corner, out of sight. I followed, just in time to see him drop a couple of pieces of cat food on the ground.

I stopped short and shouted, "Fred! We forgot all about Fred!"

Chapter 30

A fox will eat one pound of food a day. But even when it is full, it doesn't stop hunting. It stores meat, berries, worms, insects, and acorns for future meals.

"You're sure it was Fred?" Mom asked. We stood in a semicircle near the shed, watching Bo push food closer to the hole.

"It was Fred," Summer insisted. "When Vern almost kicked him, he shot back under there."

"Don't crowd around," I whispered. "Fred might be too scared to come out."

Cruuuuuck! Cruuuuuck! Bo seemed to coax. "Come out! Come out!"

Fred's black-and-white face appeared, his bright green eyes darting to each of us.

"See?" Molly cried.

Fred meowed, crawling out. He circled Bo before eating a couple of pieces of the food the raven had brought. Deep-sounding purrs of happiness were heard as Fred greeted each of us, allowing one pat, before sitting down and meowing loudly.

"You must be hungry!" I exclaimed, reaching out to pick him up.

But Fred scooted away, sat, and meowed again.

Bo walked over and dropped a few more pieces of cat food at Fred's feet.

Packrat took out his camera. "Can't believe I'm seeing a bird feed a cat."

"So that's why you kept stealing Cat Lady's cat food!" I said to the raven.

"Cooper!" Mom scolded. "Her name is Mrs. Nichols. And she's been worried sick about Fred. I can't wait to tell her—"

"*Shhhh!*" Molly put a finger to her lips. She crawled toward the hole and put her ear to it. Her eyes opened wide. "Fred?"

She plunged her hand inside the hole before anyone could stop her. "Don't—" Mom cried.

But Molly, eyes twinkling, didn't listen. She pulled something from the dark space, cuddled it for a moment, then showed us all.

A tiny black-and-white face, eyes closed, nestled in the crook of her arm.

Dad and Mom looked at each other and burst out laughing.

Fred watched as I helped Molly pull more kittens from their hiding spot, never letting them out of his—her—sight. The second one was all black, then a black-and-white one with more white than black, and finally, an orange tiger.

"Four!" Molly said.

"Guess I'll get one of those cat carriers," Roy said, heading into the shed.

"The heck with the cat carrier!" Summer exclaimed, gently picking up the orange kitten and snuggling it under her chin.

I swore I heard her whisper, "I think I'll call you Kit."

Mom and Dad led my friends and me down the red-blazed trail, taking us back to the campground. If anyone had passed us, they would have raised their eyebrows at the sight. Molly walked between my parents, murmuring to the tiny kitten in her arms. Mom held Fred. I held Oscar, and my friends all had kittens. Dad said we looked like a walking pet store.

Funny thing was, no one even thought to put the pets in the cat carriers Roy and Packrat were carrying back.

Warden Kate stayed behind at the water tower with Vern, giving details of the incident to the authorities, who'd shown up soon after she called them. She'd decided to keep Bo with her for now, until they could figure out what to do with him. When she petted his chest with her pointer finger and talked softly to him, he puffed up his feathers. I swear he would have purred, if he could have; he was in good hands.

"How'd you know where to find us?" I asked Summer, who was cooing to the kitten in her arms. She and Kit already seemed quite attached. I wouldn't want to be in her house if she asked to keep it and her dad said no.

Summer shrugged her shoulders, not quite meeting my eyes.

"Your mom told me about the note you'd left—how you'd gone to see the kits with Molly. When you weren't in the blind, I just guessed you'd be at the water tower."

She snuggled Kit under her chin, into her neck, and lifted her eyes to mine.

"I wanted to explain. That my dad wasn't a kit napper."

I rolled my eyes. I knew that *now*!

"He's a taxidermist. He preserves animals that are already dead; he doesn't kill them."

"You said he was an artist." I raised an eyebrow.

"That wasn't a lie! Getting those animals to look realistic? That's an art! He wants people to think they're real when they first see them, do a double take, you know. He sells them. Enters them in contests. Displays them. And the coolest thing? He gives them to game wardens like Warden Kate, so she can go to schools and show kids. He's good." Her eyes pleaded with me to understand. "Really good."

"Good?" I exclaimed. "He's amazing! I thought they were real!" I sighed. "It was just kinda, like, a shock, you know? Being a taxidermist is cool. It's only because you lied and tried to keep it from me that I thought you and he had anything to do with the foxes going missing." I bumped my shoulder against hers. "I'd like to see him work sometime," I said. And I meant it.

"But," I had to know, "why didn't you tell me?"

Roy and Packrat, who'd been walking in front of us, slowed down to join us. I nodded their way.

"Or them?"

Summer ran her fingers down the back of the kitten's head.

"Because you guys were all about saving animals. Protecting them. I wanted you to know that I'm into that, too, before you figured out that my house was full of dead ones." She whispered into the kitten's fur, "I've never even had a real live pet."

Packrat looked over his shoulder. "Never?"

Summer shook her head. "My dad's afraid they'll get into his work. Attack the animals, 'cause they look real and all. I keep telling him that if we train one properly—"

"Then how are you going to talk him into keeping Kit?" Roy asked.

Summer grinned. "I'm not. If Mrs. Nichols lets me adopt Kit, when he's ready, I'll keep him at my mom's place. She has a farm only twenty minutes from here, and I spend half of my summer with her. Lots of weekends, too. It's why Dad and I moved here. The drive between their houses used to be two hours, and they both started grumbling about it. So I told Dad we should live closer. So I could see her more, and be in the car less."

Packrat gave me a you-could-have-told-me look. I shrugged my shoulders. Later, I'd tell him that if he'd gotten to know Summer first, he would have found all that out.

I looked up the trail to see Mom and Dad standing in the road, waiting by our entrance sign. Summer, Packrat, and Roy moved on ahead, talking amongst themselves, Molly trailing behind. Dad and Mom fell into step on either side of me.

"Cooper," Dad began, "before we get back to the office, I wanted to say that we've asked an awful lot of you these last few days."

I shook my head no, but he kept talking.

"Even though everything isn't as perfect as we normally want it to be on Opening Day, we want you to know we'd never have gotten as far as we have without you and your friends."

I petted Oscar between the eyes, not wanting to see the disappointment in Dad's.

"I'm sorry. We coulda been ready. I had a plan, honest, I did! The four of us were going to open the spigots yesterday, after we opened the bathrooms. We could have done it in an hour, if I hadn't had a fight with Summer and found out another kit had been poached. We could have raked today, and had—"

"Cooper." Dad got down on one knee and took me by the shoulders, Mom standing behind him. "Buddy. If you'd stuck to your plan, the kits would be long gone by now. You did the right thing." Hearing Mom's clearing-her-throat noise, he quickly said, "Well, maybe not the climbing up the water tower and zip-lining part. We'll be talking about that later. But we can welcome the *Camping with the Kings* show and our early customers without the raking. And the flowers. And the rest. We'll call it our 'rustic spring look.' "

"They aren't gonna buy that, Dad!" I looked at the treetops, my sneakers, the gate, anywhere and everywhere but at him. "I promised to make things right! I wanted everything to be perfect. Just like you would have done. If I hadn't broken the Rule of Two. If I'd had your back."

Dad dipped his head lower, making me look him in the eye. His voice rose a little.

"You *did* have my back! You called for help, and you stayed with me until it came. And you accomplished so much in just a few days." He took a deep breath, lowering his voice again. "Cooper. Listen to me, son. What happened out there, it was *my* fault. I take full blame for it. And I've done nothing but lie in that hospital bed and regret not waiting for you to come back before I cut that tree."

I did look him in the eye then.

"No! Don't forgive me just because I'm your kid and you have to. It's my fault! I told everyone *you* ignored the Rule of Two, but it was really me." I poked myself in the chest. "*I* didn't come right back. *I* stopped at the foxes. *I* didn't pay attention. And—"

"It's *my* fault." This time, it came from Mom.

Dad and I looked up as she looked at us, tears in her eyes.

"Your fault?" I didn't get it. "Now *you're* trying to make me feel better! You weren't even there when the tree fell."

Mum tucked a piece of loose hair back behind her ear.

"Your father didn't think we had enough time to open early, remember? I pushed him, even got you on my side, because I thought our campground would be famous, if I could just get us on that show. Soooo, he was in a hurry to cut those trees that morning. And he was willing to risk doing it by himself to make my dream of being on the show happen."

Suddenly, I got it. We all blamed ourselves. Each one of us felt guilty—felt like we alone were to blame for Dad's accident. When really, it was just that.

An accident.

Dad stood up.

"We all made mistakes that day. But I'm here and I'm strong, thanks to you and Summer and your quick thinking. We'll also be open on time, thanks to you and your friends. Even if everything isn't perfectly perfect."

Chapter 31

*Young female foxes who do not have their own kits
yet sometimes become helpers, guarding, feeding, and
playing with their parents' new kits.*

We stepped out of the woods and into the driveway, passing through the gate as a group. Chatting and laughing and planning, it took us a while to realize we could hear voices up ahead, in what should have been an almost-empty campground. High and low, raised and murmuring, it was like a crowd or something. Dad and I looked at each other and picked up the pace. Had news reporters come to do a story? Was there another emergency?

We turned the corner to enter the campground.

"Here they come!" called a voice I didn't recognize.

The first thing I saw was the ginormous golden motorhome parked next to the store. There was a picture painted on one side of it, with mountains, a lake, a soaring eagle, and lots of trees. Right through the middle of the picture were the words CAMPING WITH THE KINGS.

Already? No! It couldn't be! It was only ten o'clock! We still had to open the spigots, clear the lines! Seeing a man with a huge camera on his shoulder, I groaned out loud. They'd even started filming already! That wasn't supposed to happen until tomorrow!

Mom bit her lower lip. My friends stopped to stare. Dad put a hand on my shoulder. "Well, Coop—"

Summer grabbed my arm and shook it. "Surprise!" Then she waved her hand high in the air, and rose on her tiptoes, calling out, "Mr. Fitzpatrick! Over here!"

I'm pretty sure my jaw hit the ground when our principal smiled and waved back. He leaned over to the cameraman, pointed at us, and the camera turned our way. Summer's and my classmates swarmed our principal, joking and laughing. A few of them waved and called out, "Hey, Cooper! Can't believe we finally get to see your place! Summer! What's up? Thanks for inviting us!"

Funny thing was, they all had rakes in their hands.

Whoa.

Stacey broke away from the crowd to rush over.

"Joan! Look! Isn't it wonderful?" She grinned from ear to ear. "It was all Summer's idea. She convinced the principal to have a community service day. Word spread, and everyone just started showing up to help! They want to rake the sites. The playground. Plant flowers. Take boats to the lake." She leaned in to wink at us, whispering, "*Camping with the Kings* is eating this up!"

I tried to take it all in, but there was so much going on! Our ice-cream delivery guy sat in the driver's seat of the dump truck, which was already half full of leaves. Ted, the camper my mom had talked to on the phone about moving campsites, drove by in his pickup, which was weighted down with boats from the rec hall. The couple we always bought our flowers from was showing a group of teachers and parents where to plant the seedlings they'd brought.

Summer's father stood handing out brushes and paint cans to a group of people painting picnic tables at the rec hall.

Even Brenda, from our post office, was sweeping the porch.

Mom had tears in her eyes. She hugged Summer so tight, I thought she'd smush the kitten. Then Mom grabbed Dad's good hand to squeeze it. He could only stare in wonder at all the people working all over our campground.

"Ice cream for everyone!" Mom called, winding her way through the crowd to the store.

"Ice cream?" Dad exclaimed. "This calls for burgers! Hot dogs! Let's fire up the grill!"

Cooper and Packrat: Mystery of the Missing Fox

There was just one more job to do. No. Wait. Feeling Oscar squirm in my hands, and hearing one of the kittens mew, I realized we had three.

First, I put Oscar in Mom's garden. He jumped right in the pond, and I swear I heard him heave a happy sigh to be back. Then Molly, my friends, and I took Fred and the kittens and began searching for Mrs. Nichols in the crowd of volunteers.

Molly ducked under someone's arm and squeezed between two customers to grab her by the hand and lead her to us. Mrs. Nichols squealed when she saw Fred. She hugged her tight, and for once, Fred let her.

"But I don't understand," she said, after we explained where Fred had been all this time, and how we'd discovered that Vern had been the one taking the fox kits. "Why would Fredericka go so far from the campground to have her kittens?"

"Fredericka?" I heard Roy whisper to Packrat. "She coulda told us that he was a she!"

Ignoring Roy, I suggested to Mrs. Nichols, "Maybe she just wanted some privacy."

"Yeah, the campground was busy with chain saws and water spraying everywhere," Roy added. "We brought back your cat carriers. They were in the shed. Vern was using them to hide the kits." Roy and Packrat placed them at her feet, and we put the kittens in one of them.

Mrs. Nichols frowned. "No, those aren't mine. Vern must have bought his own."

"Well, I guess they're yours now," I said.

I saw Warden Kate making her way through the crowd toward us, Bo on her shoulder. I still had questions for her. I hoped her team would be able to catch Vern's buyer, for one thing.

Bo flew from the warden to Mrs. Nichols's shoulder and dipped his beak so he and Fred could bump foreheads. Mrs. Nichols's voice was soft and kind, as she looked to the raven on her shoulder.

"I'm so sorry I chased you away from the cat food all those times. I should have suspected something was amiss." Mrs. Nichols tossed her long brown braid behind her, closed her eyes, and sighed.

"Aren't you happy?" Summer asked, peeking through the slats of the cat carriers, which now held all the kittens."They're so cute!"

"Yes, but I feel bad."

"Why?" I asked.

Mrs. Nichols opened her eyes.

"Because I'm the one who took your trail cam—when I put the urine-soaked T-shirt and sneakers next to the den. I didn't want you to see me doing it, and I didn't see the camera until I'd already walked in front of it. It's at my camper . . . I'm sorry for trying to drive the foxes away. Please forgive me. I was wrong. I promise to make it up to you, by helping today."

I knew all about that kind of promise.

"Time to open the spigots?" Roy asked, as Mrs. Nichols walked away with her cats and carriers, Bo still on her shoulder.

"Only if you have a poncho," Summer said, raising her chin in challenge to Packrat.

"What?" My friend widened his eyes. Looking offended, he said, "Don't you trust me?"

Summer put her hands on her hips. "Not if you have that Super Soaker in your coat!"

Packrat laughed out loud and opened it up wide so she could see he didn't.

My three friends walked ahead of me to the beginning of the water line. Summer and Roy started arguing over where the best fishing spot was on the lake.

"We'll have to have a fishing contest," Roy told Summer. "Last one to catch a bass has to cluck like a chicken from the top of the climber on Memorial Day Weekend in a chicken suit. Aaaand, do the chicken dance!"

I watched Roy wink at Packrat behind Summer's back, and I chuckled.

"I wonder what our next adventure will be?" I heard Packrat ask Roy.

I didn't care what it was.

As long as I had the three of them to watch my back.

Acknowledgments

If you'd asked me a couple of years ago what wild animal I planned to use in Cooper's third adventure, I wouldn't have hesitated in my answer: black bears. They've always been a love of mine, and the thought of spending many months researching and (dare I hope) staring at one through the lens of my camera filled me with excitement. "But," I would have told you, "I don't reeeeeally want to run into one in the wild."

Then one sunny April day in 2013, I put a lasagna in the oven and looked at my watch. I had an hour to kill before my parents arrived for dinner. So I told my husband I was going for a quick walk to grab the memory card from my trail camera. You see, there was this hole in a hill with a newly made dirt shelf, so I'd strapped the trail camera to a tree trunk and pointed it straight at that hole. So far, the camera had picked up skunks, fishers, foxes, and coyotes walking by, but not going *in*. I was sooooo curious to see what lived there.

Sound familiar, dear reader?

That day, like Cooper, I was late getting home. Watching the five kits wrestle, nip each other's ears, and tumble head over tail down the hill kept me rooted to the spot, snapping photo after photo. Luckily, my husband and parents are very forgiving, knowing what a nature geek I am. They even held supper for me, and let me ramble on and on and on about my find, and how those kits would be the perfect wildlife subject for Cooper's third adventure.

I was in love, and went on to research foxes firsthand during the next three breeding seasons, bears forgotten (though not for long).

It took more than my own research to create *Mystery of the Missing Fox*, though. From that day in the woods to writing these acknowledgments, so many people have given me encouragement, advice, gentle redirection, and inspiration to keep me going. Please indulge me while I thank some of them here. And as always, if I forget anyone, please forgive me. I do appreciate you all.

Children's writers are an extremely giving and nurturing bunch. My circle of online and in-person writing friends are no exception, especially my Camp 'n' Schmooze attendees: Carrie Jones, Val Giogas, Mona Pease, Jo Knowles, Denise Ortakales, Cindy Faughnan, Megan Frazer Blakemore, Laura Hamor, Jeanne Bracken, Nancy Cooper, Anna Jordan, Mary Morton Cowan, and Joyce Johnson. Thanks for all you do! This series might never have been born without your combined encouragement and support. I live for our Schmoozes.

A special shout-out to Schmoozer Cindy Lord, my kayaking buddy. At the eleventh hour, when I was running late on a deadline and panicking, wondering if the idea was "good enough," you made time in your busy schedule to read it and get me back on track. That meant the world to me. Thank you, my friend.

And Sammie, too, who did an entire read-through in one day! I asked, dear niece, and you didn't hesitate. Hugs!

The minute my young campers learned Cooper's third adventure would be about foxes, they had stories to share and sightings to report. It got so I had to keep a special notebook behind the camp office counter to record them all. Foxes accused of killing chickens, only to find out it was a dog. Foxes living under their front steps, crossing their driveways, or shrieking like babies behind their campsites. Each amazing story gave me insight into fox behavior, and I soaked them all up. I'm especially grateful to one of my former seasonals, Henry Farrington, who had a fox report each time he bought a morning paper from me. I felt better, Henry, knowing you were watching over them as they cut through your site in those twilight hours.

I'm blessed to work in school district RSU 16, where staff, students, and administration have been so very supportive of my writing adventures, in particular at Bruce M. Whittier Middle School in Poland, Maine, where I teach. Whether just asking how my writing is going, or when throwing Cooper and Packrat a book launch, they make me feel like a rock star, especially the students in Mrs. Shannon Shanning's room, who inspire me as I write alongside them. You are some of the most creative authors I've ever had the pleasure of working with. Never stop writing!

When it came to all the little details about head injuries, hospital stays, broken arms, and emergency protocol, I turned to the amazing men and women who teach Shannon's and my students through our Integrated Learning Program: the Midknight Fire Slayers. I'm not sure who enjoys the weekly trips to the Poland Rescue and Fire Department more, the students or me! Knot tying, hose drills, CPR and First Aid . . . we learn something new all the time! So naturally, when I knew Cooper's dad had to have a horrible accident, I turned to all of you to help me save him: Chief Mark Bosse, Captain Lee O'Connor, Private Matt Magill, Private Lisa Albee, Private Jolene Adams, Lieutenant Justin Carver, Captain Tom Printup, and Captain Shawn Hazelton. Thank you so much for your kindness and patience in answering my many questions. There will be more; Cooper just can't stay out of trouble!

Shannon, you amaze me with all you do. Always positive. Always creating. Thank you for your support in and out of the classroom. And especially for teaching Cooper and Packrat right under my nose! How many authors get to experience that? I'm honored to work with you.

Carl DiRocco, I thought the loons and eagles were amazing, but these fox kits! They're so wicked adorable! I bet every reader cries, "Awwww!" like I did, when they see them. Thank you!

Melissa Kim, my amazingly patient editor—you were right there for me, from the what-if stage, through the plotting and cutting, to the final kick in the butt I needed to wrap up this adventure. It means so much to me to be part of the Islandport family. A huge thank you, to each and every one of you, including kid reader Ryan, for loving and believing in Cooper and Packrat as much as I do.

Cooper and Packrat: Mystery of the Missing Fox

Melissa Hayes, you wrapped everything up into a tidy little package with your precise copyediting skills. I always feel better knowing you've read Cooper's adventure through and through.

I hear you, my large, boisterous, adorable family, as you cheer me on from near and far. You were all soooo relentless in asking, "Are you done yet?," too. Such an impatient lot! Well, here it is, finally. I sure hope it was worth the wait (xoxo).

Alexandra and Benjamin, if you'd been in Cooper's place, I know you'd have done the same for your dad and me. Probably more. It's why I adore you so much! Always know your dad and I are here for you. We've got your back. No matter what. Love ya.

And David: Thank you for trudging through the snow to look at water towers with me when I doubted myself and my idea, and for drawing diagrams of water spigots and valves. But mostly, thank you for always being there, beside me. I honestly don't know what I'd do without you.